Serenade

SAMANTHA MICHAELS

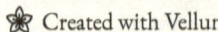

First and foremost, thank you to my husband for helping me navigate my medical issues this year. I wish I could say our challenges were over, but we'll keep fighting.

To my amazing rescue dog Holly, having you home with me not leaving my side during my recovery helped in ways you'll never know. I love you, Fuzzy-Bottoms.

To the team at Carxander Publishing, thank you for waiting for me to come back!

As always, thank you to those who take the time to read and share my work!

And a HUGE thank you to the doctors and nurses who cared for me and helped me get better. Not all heroes wear capes.

Foreword

As you read the medical issues that our female lead went through, you'll understand how the year of 2024 started for me. It wasn't an easy journey, but I made it back and better than ever.

Then in July, the world came crashing down. You won't read that in this book as the journey is just beginning, but I will tell the story some day.

It's going to be my toughest battle so far, and I'm going to need some help, but I will win this one too.

Tammy's ex-husband does not in any way represent my husband. He was and still is amazing. The negative things her ex says are all things I said to myself. I'm working on that, but it takes time to have self-confidence, especially when you never have.

Prologue

Three Years Ago
Tammy

"Nine-one-one, what's the address of your emergency?" The soothing voice on the other end of the phone asks.

"One twenty-three High Street," I say.

"And your name?"

"Tammy Foster."

"Okay, Ms. Foster. What's the nature of your emergency?"

"I woke up with severe pain in my abdomen. It's more intense than anything I've ever felt."

"I'm sorry to hear that. Help is on the way. Please stay on the line until they arrive."

"It hurts so much!" I cry out.

"Focus on my voice. Take slow, deep breaths. In through your nose, out through your mouth."

I start to feel a little more calm as I breathe, but it's not helping the pain. Several minutes later, I hear a knock on the door.

"EMTs are here," I say.

"I hope you feel better." The operator disconnects as I open the door for the EMTs.

The EMTs introduce themselves as Gary and Tony.

"Are you able to walk out to the stretcher?" Gary asks after they do their examination and determine I need to go to the hospital.

"Yes."

"You'll need to bring a photo ID and your medical insurance card. I'd also recommend bringing your cell phone."

I grab what I need and put it in a plastic bag. Gary and Tony help me walk outside. I'm thankful my porch only has two steps. I lay down on the stretcher and look up and the gray sky just as a light drizzle dampens my face. At least the rain will hide the tears from my pain and my fear. Tony gets in the driver's seat of the ambulance while Gary climbs in back with me.

"Is there anyone you need to call?"

"I need to let my husband know, but I'm in too much pain to talk. If I dial, will you tell him?"

"Yes, of course," Gary says.

I dial Martin's number and hand the phone to Gary. Gary puts the phone on speaker so I can hear the conversation.

"Hello," Martin says.

"Mr. Foster, my name is Gary. I'm a paramedic. We're currently taking your wife to the hospital."

"She called and told me she was having pain and thought she might call. I'll be there as soon as I can."

"Thank you, sir. She's in good hands until then."

The phone disconnects, and I try to relax for the rest of the drive, but the pain is severe. Gary puts an IV into my arm as he tells me a saline drip is routine. We pull into the ER parking lot. Gary and Tony wheel me to an empty ER bay. The pain's so bad, all I can do is cry.

An ER aide comes in to get me into a gown and check me in. A nurse gives me an injection of pain medication, but it does nothing to even reduce the agony in my abdomen. A short time later, Martin comes in. He's so sweet, moving his chair next to my bed and holding my hand.

"Mrs. Foster, we need to take you for an MRI. Do you have any jewelry on?" the aide asks.

"Just my rings. I'll give them to my husband."

I take my rings off, and Martin puts them in his pocket. They wheel my bed to the MRI room and transfer me to the table. The pain is unbearable, and I cry out. When the test is finally done, tears are streaming down my face as they wheel me back to the ER. A while later, a nurse comes in.

"The ER doctor reviewed your MRI and found a pocket of air in your belly. We need to take you for a CT scan to determine why."

"Ugh. The MRI was really painful. But I know it's necessary, so I'll do it."

I fade in and out as I'm wheeled somewhere. I'm vaguely aware of being moved to a table again, but I don't feel pain this time. When I'm done, I get wheeled to a hallway since my ER bay was needed for someone else.

A while later, my nurse, Kevin, comes to tell me they reviewed my CT scan. I have a perforation in my colon and a bleeding ulcer in my stomach.

"You need emergency surgery. I'm going to take you to the OR for prep, but first I need you to sign this consent form."

He reviews the form with Martin and me, then I sign. I say goodbye to Martin as they wheel me away. They put a mask on me to put me under.

When the ICU nurse finally woke me, it's nine days later...

Chapter One

"Wat the hell?" I shout as the alarm on my phone wakes me out of a dead sleep. I drag my ass out of bed for another fun day at the office. Halfway to the bathroom, my brain catches up.

"I'm retired." My first day of retirement, and I forget. I shuffle back to bed and get another hour of sleep. Once I get up, I workout and shower, then head to the kitchen for breakfast. I wander around my entire house, and I never really noticed before how lonely it is.

My mind goes back to that night, a couple of weeks after the retirement banquet. I was finally starting to make some headway with Tammy, or so I thought. Then, she withdrew again. So, I showed up at her apartment with my guitar and sang to her. It took three songs before she finally opened the door. But even then, the best I could get was friendship.

My house is two floors plus a finished basement that I use as a movie and game room and an attached garage. The basement has a pool table, ping-pong table and a sixty-inch television. I have four leather recliners with cup holders and built in massagers. I also have a state-of-the-art sound system, so I never need to go to the movies. There's also a bar, a fridge, and a half-bath.

The outside facade is stone with a full length porch and double doors to enter. After a small foyer, the kitchen is to the right and includes a door to the garage and a second half-bath. As you continue, you walk through an alcove, you reach the dining room. Finally, a second alcove takes you to the living room, complete with sliding glass doors that lead to a massive, fenced-in backyard.

The second floor has a long hallway with a u-shape of rooms. One side features three bedrooms. Across the hall are two more rooms, one that's my secret music room, and one that's a workout room, plus there's a full bathroom. The bathroom has a large shower stall and a heated hot tub for two. Now, if only I had a second to join me.

But not just any second.

One particular second.

Tammy.

Finally, the smaller part of the u is my home office.

I can't help but feel lost. I've been working for all of my adult life. To all of a sudden have that gone is leaving me feeling helpless. I need to find something to fill my days. I've always wanted a dog, but I never thought it was fair with the hours I work. Correction. Worked.

I'm about to head down to our local shelter to find a friend to bring home when my cell rings. I see Tammy's pretty face on my screen. I snapped this picture at my friend Mel's wedding. Tammy was dancing, and the look of joy on her face took my breath away.

Her image floats through my head. Her fiery, long, red hair goes perfectly with her bright, emerald-colored eyes. Her creamy complexion is stunning, and I love the cute smattering of freckles on her nose. She's curvy in all the right places and damn, I bet she looks amazing sans clothing. What impresses me most, though, is her height. Like my friend Mel, Tammy's tall. Five foot eight or nine, if I had to guess. I like having a woman who doesn't have to stand on her tiptoes to see my face.

"Hey, Tam. What's up?"

I hear sniffles, but no words.

Finally, I barely hear, "Can I come over?"

"Of course. I'll be sitting out back."

She disconnects without another word. I fix two cups of iced coffee, her favorite, and take them out to the back porch. Tammy arrives, plops down in one of the chairs, and takes a small sip of coffee.

"Thank you," she says, pointing at the cup.

"My pleasure. Now, tell me, what's wrong?" I look at the tear-stained face of my friend and feel like I'm being stabbed in the heart. Her beautiful green eyes have lost their shine, and it kills me.

"Nick's retiring, and he's looking to sell the Full Moon. I can't lose my job."

"I'm so sorry, but maybe a new owner would keep you on."

"I asked Nick when he broke the news. All he would say was that he couldn't guarantee anything. I know what that means."

I gently run my hand along her arm, trying to comfort her. My wheels start spinning. But I don't say anything. "Well, maybe it will work out."

"But what if it doesn't? I don't have much to fall back on. Martin made sure of that in the divorce."

"Do you have to work tonight?"

"No, he's closing tonight so he can get professional cleaners in. The place needs to look its best for potential buyers.

"Well, how about we hang out? I was just getting ready to head somewhere that I know will be a good distraction."

"I could use that. Count me in. I'm so lucky you're my friend."

Damn, that felt like a kick in the gut. I love being friends with Tammy and getting to know more about her, though I suspect she's still holding a lot back. But lately, I want more. I'm falling for this woman, but I can't seem to break through that shell of hers.

We head out to my truck. "Where are we goin'?"

"It's a surprise."

"Hmmm. Should I be scared or excited?"

I flash a wicked smile, but refuse to spoil the destination. She squeals and claps when she sees me pull into the shelter parking lot.

"I've always wanted a dog, but with my hours, it wouldn't have been fair to leave her or him alone that long. But now, nothing is holding me back."

I walk around to her side and help her down. We walk inside and up to the desk.

"May I help you?" a young lady named Piper asks.

"I'm here to adopt a dog," I say. Piper's eyes fill with tears. "Are you okay?" I ask.

"Oh yes, sorry. We've had several surrenders today, so having you come to adopt is music to my ears. Let me get Carly, our adoption manager, and she'll take you to the kennels.

"Thank you."

Carly comes out and takes Tammy and me to the back.

"Piper mentioned you had quite a few surrenders today. That makes me sad."

"Me too. And one is going to be next to impossible to adopt."

"Why's that?"

"Most people only want one dog, but this is a bonded pair of siblings. Two one-year-old female pure-bred black labs."

"And they were surrendered? Labs are so sweet. Friends of ours have two that they found abandoned in the park."

"Oh, we heard that story. I'm so glad your friends found them."

"Could I see the labs?"

"Sure. They're in one of the exam rooms until we make room in the kennel." Carly looks down at her feet, and my breath catches in her throat.

"I don't wanna know how you make room, do I?"

Carla shakes her head back and forth.

"Have you considered an adoption fair?"

"We can't afford it. Donations are at an all-time low. Anything we get goes to the care of the animals we have."

"What if someone sponsored it?"

"You know someone?"

"Yeah. Me. How soon can you organize it?"

"We can do it as early as this weekend."

"Tell me how much you need. Oh, and I will adopt the two labs."

"Thank you so much. I'll waive your adoption fee as a thank you."

"I won't hear of it."

"You also get one year of free vet services."

"Please, put that money into your other animals or adopters who need the financial help."

"Mr., um, I apologize. I never asked your name."

"Jason Donnelly, but I go by Jay."

"Well, Mr. Donnelly, you've certainly brightened what was going to be a very tough day here."

Carly grabs a clipboard and hands it to me. "Please fill this out to adopt the girls."

I fill out the paperwork and hand it back to Carly. Piper processes everything, and I pay my adoption fee, adding a little extra to help. I glance over at Tammy, and her eyes are filled with tears.

"These ones are happy," she says, smiling.

Carla brings the girls out, and it takes me a millisecond to fall in love with them. Carla can't stop grinning as she watches Tammy and me with the dogs.

What a great family we'd be.

Where the hell did that just come from? I push the thought aside.

"Now, tell me how much you need for the fair."

"Let's talk in my office."

"Do you mind if I take the girls outside and walk a bit?" Tammy asks me.

"Of course not." I follow Carly into her office as Tammy takes the dogs.

"I hope this isn't too much, but the last fair we did was fifteen thousand."

"Very well." I take my checkbook out of my jacket pocket and hand her a check for twenty thousand.

"Are you sure? It likely won't cost this much."

"Then the rest is for care of future animals, though my goal is to not have any here after this weekend. I have some friends who own popular local businesses, and I know they'll help me advertise. Especially my friends Mikael and Hannah, who own a pet supply shop."

"I'm truly beside myself."

"My pleasure. And you can count on me to volunteer as well."

"Great. I have your contact info from your paperwork, so I'll be in touch with all the details."

"Looking forward to it."

"Enjoy the girls, and thank you again for adopting them."

I nod and smile, then head outside to join Tammy. "Wanna do some shopping with me?"

"I'd love to."

After we buy out half the pet supply store, we take the girls back to my house and take them into the backyard.

"The girls need names," I say. "I'd love for you to name one of them."

"Are you sure?"

"Damn right."

"Yay! I think the names should go together somehow."

"Okay, don't tell anyone I'm admitting this, but I have a favorite show that would be perfect! So, I'm naming one of the girls Lorelei."

"Eeeekkkk!" Tammy squeals. "I love that show. I didn't know you were such a softie. Sookie it is."

"Another thing we have in common. We need a binge night sometime."

"Ooooh. Count me in!"

"It's a date."

Chapter Two

Tammy

I *t's a date.*

Jay's words run through my head for the thousandth time. I've been sensing for a while that Jay wants to be more than friends. But that means intimacy, and I just can't let him see me. I wish I could tell him. Make him understand why this terrifies me. He'll think less of me if I do. Martin told me nobody would love me unless I kept *it* hidden. So dammit, that's what I'm gonna do.

And, of course, now, Jay's floating through my head. Talk about delicious. He's six feet of pure heaven. His dark brown hair and light coffee-colored eyes are stunning. I could get lost in those eyes. And damn, that man fills out a pair of jeans and a tee-shirt like nobody I've ever laid eyes on. He definitely works out! I blush when I try to imagine how he must look in all his naked glory.

My little Westie, Sadie, lays on the floor at my feet, watching me get ready. I scratch her head, and she flops on her side. "Am I crazy?" I ask her. She rubs her head against me, and I remember why I'm so lucky to have her. She'll never judge me. She just loves me, especially when I feed her! I was so grateful to find an apartment that allowed pets.

Even though the Saloon is still closed, Nick called us all in to take inventory. He's paying us, but it's not the same. People tend to be more generous with tips the more they have to drink, and I'm struggling without the extra money. I'm trying not to panic, as I try to decide what to do next.

So far, there's been no word on any potential buyers. I don't handle uncertainty well, especially when it comes to my well-being. Just when things are starting to look up, this happens, and now I have no idea how long I'll have a job.

Nick hands out assignments, putting me in charge of counting glasses. I have my back turned to the front door when I hear Nick greet someone. I'd swear it was Jay's voice, but why would he be here? By the time I turn, nobody's there, so I shake my head and get back to work. After I finish, I grab my purse from my locker and head out to my car.

Before I pull out of the lot, I check my phone, and I have a text from Jay.

Hey, doll. Wanna have dinner at my house tonight? Lorelei and Sookie miss you.

I text him back. *I'll be there. What time, and what can I bring?*

Five, and just that pretty smile.

I sent back an emoji of a face blushing.

****

I pull into Jay's driveway a little before five. I can hear him out back with the dogs, so I join him. The girls run over to me as soon as they notice me. Jay joins them and gives me a hug. Electric sparks run through my veins and I want nothing more at that moment than to feel his lips on mine.

No.

That cannot happen.

An argument erupts inside my head.

Just tell him. He'll understand.

No he won't.

Yes he will.

I can't tell him.

Then show him, you coward.

12

I could never do that. He'd be horrified.
You're an idiot. He's a great guy.
Too great for me.
Whatever.
Right back at you.

Jay's voice ends the argument. "Earth to Tammy. Where were you?"

"Sorry, a lot on my mind. I'm so scared about losing my job."

"Well, then you especially want to listen."

"Listen to what?"

"You heard nothing that I said, did you?"

"Guilty. I'm so sorry."

"No worries."

Jay pauses. He stands there gazing at me, and I let out a nervous giggle. He's gonna think I'm a dork.

"Well? Don't keep me waiting."

In tones so hushed, I can barely hear him. "I bought the Saloon."

I freeze in place as my jaw hits the floor. "W-w-what did you just say?"

He repeats himself with more volume this time, "I bought the Saloon."

"If I had a thousand guesses of what you wanted to tell me, that would not have been one of them. I'm almost afraid to ask, but what does that mean for the bar?"

"I think what you should be asking is what does that mean for you."

"Well, I do wanna know, but I'm scared. So, let me have it. Do I get to keep my job?"

"Nope."

My heart sinks to the floor. How can he do this to me? Tears sting my eyes, and I can't stop them from spilling over. I sink to my knees, burying my head in my hands. My body shakes as I move from tears to full-on sobs.

I feel a presence next to me. Lifting my head, Jay's on his knees next to me.

"Tam, I'm so sorry. That was so much better in my head."

"What, you enjoyed destroying my life in your head?"

13

"No, no, it's not like that." His hand lifts my chin a little more, and I gaze into his eyes. There's a softness that makes me feel better.

"Then what? You know damn well losing my job would ruin me. How could you do this to me?"

"Please, let me explain. What I meant, and so royally fucked up, was to tell you I'm offering you a different job."

"Really? So, I won't be a waitress anymore?"

"Is that okay?"

"Oh, yes. Don't get me wrong, I've loved waitressing, but it takes a toll on you after a while."

"I'm sure. What I need is a manager to oversee the waitresses. You'll be the boss, and the promotion will come with a significant salary increase."

"I mean, are you sure? I'm not educated."

"What do you mean?"

"Well, I graduated high school, but nothing else."

"Listen to me, education isn't one size fits all. You've worked at the Saloon for what, thirty-five years, Nick told me?"

"Yeah."

"So, who knows the place better than you?"

"Well, yeah, I know the job, but maybe some courses would help me."

"Tell ya what, if you want to take some classes, I'll pay."

"No, I could never accept that just because we're friends."

I see his lips tighten when I say that. "That's not the reason. I'm going to offer it to the entire staff."

"Wow. That's amazing. I've heard a couple of the other waitresses saying they'd like to change careers, but just couldn't afford a degree program."

"Great. I'll need some time to get some things in order, then Nick and I will hold a meeting to announce the sale. I just need to ask that you keep things confidential until then."

"Of course. I really can't thank you enough. It feels like the weight of the world has been lifted off my shoulders."

"I can see the difference in that beautiful face."

My cheeks heat up. He really needs glasses if he thinks *I'm* beautiful.

I believe the last thing Martin said to me was, 'You fat, ugly pig'. And that's the only thing I'll ever believe.

"So, do you accept? I need a verbal yes."

"Yes, I do. And I can't tell you how beyond grateful I am."

"My pleasure." He licks his lips when he says that, and my entire body heats up. "Now, I'd love to enjoy a meal with the most beautiful woman I've ever laid eyes on."

Tears sting my eyes. I grab my purse and pull my car keys out. I knew he had to have someone. A good looking man like him would never be alone. "Well, enjoy. Just call me when you're ready for me to report to The Saloon."

"I beg your pardon? Where are you goin'?"

"Home. I don't want to disrupt your evening."

"You lost me. I thought we were gonna have dinner."

"So did I, but then you said you were gonna enjoy a meal with a beautiful woman, so I know that's my cue to leave."

"Tam, you're a beautiful woman."

"Oh, please. I'm as ugly a woman as you'll ever see."

"Who told you that? Because they need their ass kicked."

"Nobody. Just forget it." Tears threaten to spill over yet again. Before they can, and before Jay can ask anymore questions, I grab my stuff and run to my car. I race out of this driveway, tires squealing as I speed away.

Chapter Three

Jay

I'm standing in my doorway dumbfounded by what just happened. Well, truth be told, I'm still not sure what happened. Tammy was so happy when I told her about the bar. So, what the hell caused that switch to flip?

I grab my phone and dial one of my favorite numbers.

"Hey, Jay, what's happening?" My best friend, Mel, asks when she answers.

"I need some advice. Would Judd mind if you joined me for coffee?"

"Not at all. Diner?"

"Where else?"

Mel giggles and replies, "On my way."

I'm so glad Mel and Judd decided to move back to town. They got lonely in their mountain home being away from all their friends. I'd be lost without her to talk to.

****

Mel's car is already in the lot when I pull into the New Holland

Family Restaurant parking lot. I head inside, and she's at our favorite booth in the back. Two coffee cups and a pot sit on the table. I smile at my friend as I sit.

"You always know exactly what I need, girl,"

"Please, after all those years at O'Laughlin, I know you better than anyone! So, tell me, what's goin' on?"

"It's Tammy."

I fill Mel in on buying The Saloon and what happened tonight. She rests one elbow on the table, her head resting on her hand as she listens to me. She covers my hand with her other hand, and I feel a little better.

"Listen, I don't need to tell you what a great guy you are. I don't think this is anything you did or said."

"Then what? I don't know what else to do. I've dropped tons of hints that I want to be more than friends, and I'm getting nowhere. Then with what happened tonight." I shrug my shoulders.

"Has she told you anything about her past?"

"I know she's divorced."

"Yeah, I remember her mentioning that once. Maybe her ex is the one that made her feel unworthy."

"That makes sense. Especially given how Doug made you feel. But how did you move past it?"

"It wasn't easy. Judd and I had quite a few bumps before I was able to fully give him my heart. Maybe he's the one you should be talking to. I can call him."

"Thanks, but I've already bugged you. I hate to bug him, too."

"Nonsense." Mel grabs her phone, sends a quick text, and a few minutes later, Judd joins us. Mel fills him in.

"First thing, man, is not to give up. If you truly want to be with Tammy, you need to make sure she knows. But, you wanna watch that you don't push too hard. Most important is helping her feel safe, so she can tell you what happened in her past," Judd says.

"How long do I wait?" I ask.

"Personally, I'd call her tonight," Judd says.

"I agree. I'd like you to call right away. Otherwise, I would think I scared you off," Mel adds.

"Thanks, you guys," I say.

"We're always here for you," Mel says. "And definitely let us know when you have the grand re-opening."

"Of course. You'll be on the VIP list," I say.

Mel and Judd finish their coffee and head home. I decided to stay at the diner a little longer. While I'm nursing another cup, I call Tammy.

"Can we talk about what happened?" I ask when she picks up.

"You still wanna talk to me?"

"Yeah. You're my friend, and I care about you."

"I guess, but just... I don't want to tonight."

"Fair enough. How about we try dinner again? But please, no comments about having dinner with a woman who looks a certain way."

"Okay." But it's not.

"See ya tomorrow."

"Goodnight."

Tammy disconnects, and after paying the check, I head home.

****

After a restless night's sleep, I head off to the grocery store to grab what I need to make a delicious meal for my girl. Well, I wish she was my girl. I'm hoping tonight will at least let me start to scratch the surface of the mystery that's Tammy's past. I grab some flowers on the way home, and a plan forms. Let's just hope it doesn't backfire.

After prepping the food, I spend the rest of the day in meetings getting things ready for the bar. Things are ahead of schedule, which is great for me, and even better for Tammy. I can't wait until I can make her a new salary offer. After I'm done, I get ready for tonight. Part of me thinks this could be the breakthrough we need, and part of me fears an implosion.

I'm just getting the chicken parmesan into the oven when I hear the doorbell, followed by dueling barks. I rub each dog's heads before I open the door, flowers in my hand. I hand them to her as the dogs run past me and right to Tammy.

"Well, I see where their loyalty lies," I tease. Tammy laughs, and I relax a bit.

"Wow, something smells divine," Tammy says as she inhales deeply. "And, thank you for the beautiful flowers."

"Befitting a woman as beautiful as you. Dinner will be ready in about forty minutes," I say. "Would you like to join me on the back patio? That way, the girls can get some running in and hopefully sleep while we eat."

"I'd love to."

Tammy seems calmer tonight. More upbeat. That gives me hope this will go better than I thought.

"Would you like something to drink?"

"By chance, do you have anything diet?"

"I'm sorry, no."

"Then water will be fine."

Note to self: do some shopping tomorrow.

I return with two waters and join her at the table.

"Thank you," she says, smiling.

"You're welcome." Now, how to approach what I want to talk about. I don't wanna just blurt it out. Suddenly, all the techniques I learned over the years at work go into hiding, and I can't think of a damn one. Guess I just need to jump in.

"Can we talk about last night?" I ask in a slightly hushed tone.

"I guess. What do you wanna know?"

"Why do you think all those bad things about yourself?"

Tammy inhales and exhales loudly. "I can't believe I'm telling you this after I swore I'd never tell a soul."

"You can trust me."

She whispers, "My ex-husband." Tears immediately spill over, staining her pretty cheeks. She lowers her head, staring at her lap. I take her hand in mine. She lifts her head and meets my gaze. "How are you not repulsed by me?"

"I hate that he said those things to you. You're beautiful, and I'm not just saying that."

Her face brightens, but as quickly as it did, her expression darkens again. She waves me off. "Yeah, well, you're wrong. There's a lot you can't see, and you never will."

"I don't understand."

"And you don't need to. Please, what I've told you tonight was a huge step for me. I can't handle anything more right now. Or ever. I don't know."

I'm about to respond when the alarm on my phone buzzes. "I need to get the pasta on."

"Would you mind if I stayed out here with the dogs for a bit?"

"Not at all."

After I get the water boiling and the pasta in, I start to head back outside. I stop when I see Tammy sitting in the grass, each dog's head resting on her lap. I can see she's talking to them, and I want to respect her privacy. I just hope someday she'll feel like she can tell me what she's telling them.

When dinner's ready, I knock on the sliding glass door. Tammy gets up, and I see her rub her stomach, a disgusted look on her face. I wonder what that's about. She rounds up the dogs, and they all head inside.

"Can I help get things ready?" she asks.

"No way. You're my guest."

She smiles as she sits at the table. I put two plates together and carry them to the table. After we eat and clean up, I walk over to my stereo and put some soft music on. I hold out my hand. Tammy hesitates before she accepts it. I pull her close, and we sway to the music. Nothing has ever felt as right as this moment.

Being a taller woman, Tammy's easily able to meet my gaze. I see something different in her eyes tonight. They seem brighter. Happier. My heart swells as I finally feel some hope. I lean forward and lightly brush her lips with mine. So soft. Her eyes widen as I deepen the kiss, and I fear she's going to pull away. She doesn't.

I feel her tongue just barely enter my mouth. I tease her tongue with mine. The heat between us could burn my entire house down. I finally know what heaven feels like.

And out of nowhere, everything goes cold.

"I can't," she whispers.

"Why not?" I ask, a bit louder than intended.

"I'm ugly. You don't want me. Please stop pretending."

"I wish I knew how to make you believe what I know is true."

"Well, you can't. Friendship is all I'll ever be capable of."

"But Tammy, that kiss."

"It was nice, but it won't happen again. Thank you for a lovely evening."

"Please, don't go."

"I have to."

And without another word, Tammy is gone. Again.

Chapter Four

Tammy

S itting in the parking lot of my apartment building, I replay the evening in my head. That kiss. Oh my god, that kiss. I never wanted it to end, but it had to. I know where it was heading and that cannot happen. Even though I want it to. But one look at me, and he'll run away screaming. Why now? Why did I have to meet this amazing man? The one who very well could be the love of my life. Maybe I should just come clean and tell him everything. That way, he can get out before he gets any closer to me. I'll definitely miss the dogs.

I grab my cell and dial. "Can I come over?" I ask him.

Jay's standing on his front porch when I pull into his driveway again. He walks over to my car, helps me out, and holds my hand as we walk inside. I sink down onto his velvety, dark blue couch and bury my head in my hands.

I feel a strong hand on my shoulder. "Talk to me. I mean, if you want."

"I do. And I need you just to listen until I'm done so I don't lose my courage. I do need to warn you, this is a long story, so please, tell me now if you'd rather not hear it."

"I want nothing more than to hear it. I need to understand you."

"Well, you will after this." I turn my body so I'm facing him. He takes my hands in his. I take a deep breath, exhale slowly, and dive in.

"It was a cold, rainy, January morning three years ago," I stop, realizing I sound like the start of every story I wrote in middle school. "I woke up with the worst abdominal pain I'd ever felt. Martin had already left for work, so I called him. I'm sure he knew I'd have to call for an ambulance. I did just that. After a long day of pain and tons of tests, they discovered I had a bleeding ulcer in my stomach, and I had to get emergency surgery."

I pause, trying to fight back the tears that are threatening to spill over. Jay lightly squeezes my hands, and I continue. "I vaguely remember waking up the next day, but I wasn't awake long. I couldn't breathe on my own, so they had to put me on a ventilator. My body, however, had other ideas, and I kept fighting it. They had to put me into a medically induced coma so the ventilator could breathe for me."

Jay looks like he wants to ask something.

"Did you have a question?"

"I can wait."

"No, please ask."

"For how long?"

"They brought me out of it nine days later."

"Wow. That must have been scary."

"It was, but that's only the beginning of the journey."

"Do you want to keep going?"

"Yeah. It was a couple of days later before I could finally talk. I had a tube down my throat, and I was also being fed via a tube. If I needed to communicate, I had to write. And because I had just been awakened, it was hard to read my writing. All Martin did was get frustrated with me. He was a saint when there were nurses in the room, but when it was just us, he was nasty,"

"With everything you'd gone through? Sorry, I couldn't help myself."

I smile at how protective he seems. "That didn't matter. He said some horrible things. Constantly told me I was a fat pig, and that's why all this happened. Now, in all honesty, I was heavy at the time that this happened. However, it wasn't just because I over-ate and was lazy like he said. I'll admit, I wasn't the healthiest eater, but my habits didn't fully explain my weight. But we'll get to that."

This time, I can't fight the tears, and they spill down my face. Jay cups my face and dries my cheeks with his thumbs. His touch is so tender, and my insides melt.

"I spent several weeks in the ICU. Physically, it wasn't bad, They had me on a lot of heavy duty pain meds. But mentally, that's another story. I spent most of my days with the TV on just staring out the window. And the way my mind wandered. Not to a good place. I was so hard on myself. The things I said to myself made things Martin said seem tame."

Jay's watching me, but he doesn't say a word.

"I was convinced this was all my fault. That I was being punished for something. I can remember some of the things I said in my head. I called myself stupid, worthless, garbage, you name it. When I was first allowed to eat, I couldn't cut my food. Instead of asking a nurse for help, I just didn't eat that night."

"Oh, Tammy," is all Jay can manage.

"Once I was stable enough, they downgraded me to PCU, which is progressive care. From there, I was discharged to a physical rehab facility to get my strength up. I finally got to go home near the end of February. Then, a couple weeks later, I was back in the hospital."

"Oh, Tammy, I don't know what to say."

"Well, just wait because this part has quite the ending."

"I'm intrigued."

"After about a week into the second stay, they took me in for a heart catheterization test. And they found something that had been missed for far too long. I had congestive heart failure, causing my body to fill with fluid. That was the biggest part of my weight gain."

"So the doctor finding that turned out to be a good thing?"

"It did, but of course, I had my bumps. Well, one big bump."

"And that was?"

"Martin served me with divorce papers."

"While you were in the hospital?" Jay exclaims.

"Yep. He said I would always be nothing more than a worthless piece of garbage, and he had no desire to take care of me anymore."

"Asshole."

"Pretty much, but at the time, it got me down on myself rather than angry at him. But back to my medical stuff for now. The cardiologist who saw me came up with a plan to treat the fluid. I spent a couple of days getting a procedure called aquapheresis. The procedure reduced the amount of fluid in my body. Once I finished that, I moved to IV diuretics, then, finally, oral. That, and completely changing the way I eat, helped me lose all the excess weight."

"Then, can I ask why you still say negative things about yourself?"

"Comments like those that came from Martin were the only thing I heard for so long, it's hard to believe anything else."

"What about your friends?"

"All my friends were from the marriage, so they all went with Martin. When I got discharged the second time, I had no home. Nick was kind enough to let me stay with him until I found an apartment. I don't know what I would have done without his support."

"I really hate how much Martin hurt you."

I nod in agreement. "As hard as all the physical stuff was, the toll it took on me mentally was almost harder. But after everything I've told you tonight, I can't talk about that, too."

"I understand."

"Part of me can't believe I told you as much as I did. But you make it easy to trust you. Please, promise you won't betray that."

"You have my word."

"Thank you," I say, finishing it with a yawn. "Sorry, I'm suddenly exhausted,"

"If you don't feel like driving home, you're welcome to stay in my guest room."

"Thanks for the offer, but I'm good."

Hw frowns but doesn't say anything. No way I can take the chance of being that close to him. He has no idea, but I left something out on purpose. That would be the thing that pushes him away, and I can never let him know. Even though that means denying myself that which I want the most.

I gather up my stuff to leave. "Thank you for dinner, and for listening to me"

"Anytime."

The dogs whimper when I leave, and it feels like someone's stabbing my heart. That's definitely a reason to stay, but I just can't.

Chapter Five

Jay

After Tammy leaves, I plop down on the couch and end up falling asleep there.

I wake up the next morning and find that my brain is having a hard time processing everything she told me. Most of all, though, I want nothing more than to beat the hell out of her ex-husband. How could anyone be so cold?

I know she said there's emotional stuff she hasn't told me yet, but I feel like that's not all. There's still something that's making her pull away. I start going back over the details in my head, and it hits me. But it's nothing I would ever ask her. I just have to hope she'll tell me.

My cell phone snaps me back to reality.

"Hello."

"Mr. Donnelly, is this a good time?"

"Yes," I say to Elliott Cavanaugh, my attorney.

"Great. I just finished up a meeting with Nick's lawyer, and everything's in order. We just need you and Nick to come in and sign all the necessary paperwork. Then, the bar is yours."

"Wonderful. Has a meeting been scheduled?"

"Can you be at the bar today at one?"

"Absolutely. Thank you."

After we disconnect, I let the dogs out for a bathroom break. I let them run while I get my breakfast ready. After filling their food bowls, we all eat. After breakfast, I run out and do some errands. My last stop is the grocery store to get some diet drinks for Tammy. I get home, grab a shower, and get dressed in khakis and a polo shirt, then head to my meeting.

After we sign all the paperwork, Nick hands me the keys and shakes my hand, "Thank you for keeping my bar going. Most importantly, thank you for keeping my staff employed."

"You're welcome. I've been here enough to see what great employees they are, so I definitely want to stay on."

"Especially Tammy, right?" Nick says with a wink.

"Uh, not sure what you mean."

"Dude, I see the way you look at her. I won't push, but just please, all I ask is that you don't hurt her."

"I promise. At least, for now, we're just friends. She said that's all she's capable of."

"I blame that asshole, Martin."

"Me too. But he'll never hurt her again."

"Thanks, Jay. You're a good man."

"As are you. She told me how you helped her when she got home from her second hospital stay."

"I just didn't have the heart to see her with nowhere to go."

"I woulda done the same."

"Well, I need to head home. The wife and I have a lot of work to do to get ready for Florida."

"Enjoy retirement."

"I definitely will."

We shake hands again before Nick and both attorneys head out. I grab my cell and call Tammy.

"Hi, Jay," she says when she answers.

Her voice is like angels singing, "I'm down at The Saloon. My new bar. That sounds so strange to say. Would you like to join me so we can talk about some things before we call the rest of the staff in?"

"On my way." The excitement in her voice is infectious, and I can't wait until we're ready for a grand re-opening. More than that, I can't wait to present Tammy with her offer sheet. I think she'll be quite pleased with her new salary.

****

I'm in the kitchen when I hear the door open. "Jay, where are you?"

I walk out and almost faint. Tammy's in jeans and a pretty yellow t-shirt. She's truly stunning. "Let's head up to my office so I can go over some stuff with you."

"Should I be nervous?"

"I don't think so. Excited, yeah, but not nervous."

She heads for the office, and I see a bounce in her step that's new. I can't help but smile. And hey, that ass is quite the sexy view! "Please have a seat," I say.

She takes the seat in front of the desk while I sit down in the fancy chair I splurged on for myself. I grab the file folder sitting on the desk and pull out the piece of paper guaranteed to change Tammy's life. I try my best to keep a straight face, but I can't. I hand her a copy of the paper and give her a few minutes.

"I-I-I think there's a mistake on this paper."

"Where?"

"The number."

"No, it's not a mistake. That's what I feel you deserve for the work I'll be asking you to do. I'm going to place quite a bit of responsibility on you, and you will be fairly compensated for that work."

"But that much? I don't deserve that."

"Give me one good reason why not."

"I'm just a waitress."

"First of all, there is no such thing as just a waitress. It's a physically demanding job, not to mention having to put up with men who've had too much to drink and forget their boundaries. Second, you will now be managing the staff, doing payroll, being in charge of inventory and ordering, among other things."

"I've never done any of this."

"I know, and I'll be training you. And I have all the confidence in the world that you'll be fine."

"You have more faith in me than I do."

"We'll work on that. Now, I need you to sign one of the copies of the offer letter, if you accept."

I hold up a pen. Hand shaking, Tammy takes it and signs the offer letter. She hands it back to me. I see a couple tears slide down her face.

"I can't thank you enough," she says with a sniffle. "I might finally be able to get out of that apartment."

"That would be great." *I really wish it was to move in with me.* "Now, how about we go enjoy a celebratory lunch, then come back and get started. I'd love to be able to open within a few weeks.

"Sounds great. Let me just run to the ladies room."

As I'm waiting for Tammy, the front door yanks open, and a man storms in. He doesn't look happy.

"May I help you, sir?"

"No, you may not. I'm here to see my fuckin' pig of an ex-wife."

It can't be. It takes every ounce of my restraint not to grab him and knock him on his ass.

"May I ask her name?"

"Tammy. Now, is she here or not, asshole?"

"I beg your pardon. I'm trying to help you. There's no need to speak to me like that."

"Fuck off. Where's Nick?"

"Nick retired. I'm the new owner, and I will not have you speaking about any member of my staff like that."

"What the fuck ever. She's nothing but a fat, worthless pig. Now, can I please oink at her, I mean talk to her?"

"No, I don't think you can. I won't have you upset her."

"It's okay, Jay," I hear Tammy whisper. "What do you want, Martin?'

"I came by to let you know that I decided to buy some real estate."

"And why would I care?"

"Because I bought the apartment building you live in."

"So, uh, you're my landlord now?"

"Nope, bitch. You're being evicted, effective immediately."

"On what grounds?"

"No pets. You and your fuckin' dirty dog can have until five today to get your shit out."

Rage fills me and I grab Martin by the shirt.

"Jay, stop, he's not worth it. But I'm gonna have to skip lunch."

"Lunch? Are you actually dating this piece of garbage?" Martin asks me.

"She's my employee. In fact, I just finished promoting her to manager."

"Her," he snorts as he points at her. "What the fuck makes her qualified?"

"Well, not that it's any of your concern, but Ms. Foster is a smart, hard-working woman. The other staff members respect her, and she'll make a great leader."

"Dude, you need your head examined, not to mention your eyes. How can you stand to look at her?"

"Looks are irrelevant in the workplace."

"Well, that's good since hers are atrocious."

"Okay, you've made your point, now please leave," I say to Martin.

"Whatever. I hope you fall on your face, pig bitch."

I look at Tammy and see an expression I've never seen before. I watch her hands ball into fists at each side of her body. Her chest puffs out, and she shouts, I mean really shouts, "I hope you get every STD known to man and your dick falls off!" I swear her fiery red hair gets brighter.

Martin turns bright red in the face. He opens his mouth, but I flash him a look that quickly changes his mind. He turns on his heel, and in all his graceful glory, trips over his own feet. He stumbles out the door, hopefully never to be seen again.

I turn to Tammy, expecting to find her in tears. Instead, she's doubled over in laughter. "I can't believe I just said that to him!"

"I'm proud of you."

Her expression turns serious. "But what am I gonna do now? I have nowhere to live."

"Tell you what, let's grab sandwiches and head to your apartment. I'll help you pack, and we'll figure things out from there."

"Oh, Jay, I can't ask you to do that. This is my problem, not yours."

"You didn't ask. Now, come on, let's go. I'll grab lunch and meet you there."

"You remember the address, right?"

"Yep, from the night I picked you up for my retirement dinner."

"Thanks, Jay. I really appreciate it."

Chapter Six

Tammy

I get inside my apartment and collapse on the couch. Why can't Martin just leave me alone? My life is finally going well, then I get punched in the gut. And now, I have no home. Sure, I was planning to move eventually. But to only have a few hours to pack up all my stuff is daunting, to say the least. How many times is Jay gonna be willing to come to my rescue?

Sadie curls up on my lap as I stroke her soft white fur. I'd be lost without her. What am I gonna do? I need to find a place to stay where I can bring her. That's gonna be tough, but I'll sleep in my car before I'll part from her.

I hear a knock on my door. "It's me, Jay."

"Come in, my lap is occupied at the moment."

Sadie looks up as Jay walks over to the couch. She looks him over, then looks at me. I swear on my life she gives me her approval. If only I could get her to understand why that will never happen. More importantly, I wish I could get Jay to understand.

And then, sweet Sadie, who's supposed to be my friend, delivers the ultimate betrayal. When she gets off my lap, one of her paws gets caught in my shirt and pulls it up. My entire scar from my surgery is showing. I sit frozen in horror waiting for Jay to drop the sandwiches and run out screaming. But he doesn't. Instead, he sits down next to me.

"Don't look at me!" I cry out, panicking and trying to fix myself.

"Why? You're beautiful."

"Oh, yeah, right. This is really fuckin' beautiful," I say, pointing at my ugly scar.

"Tammy, is this why you've been fighting your feelings for me?"

"Who said I have feelings for you?"

"I can feel it. Please, tell me. Is this your hesitation?"

"Yeah," I whisper. "I'm hideous. Nobody will ever want to be intimate with me when they see this."

Jay takes my hands. "I want you to listen to me. You are the furthest thing from hideous that I've ever laid eyes on."

"But the scar-"

"Stop. Let me tell you what the scar says to me. It tells me that you're a badass who survived one hell of a medical ordeal. And during that ordeal, your asshat of an ex-husband divorced you. While you were still in the hospital. When I see that scar, I see strength. I see a fighter. I see a woman who didn't give up. And that's the sexiest damn thing I can think of."

"I'll admit that's nice to hear after everything *he* said earlier. I always thought of my scar as something to be embarrassed about."

"Even when those scars don't yield the results we want, you should still feel proud."

I notice Jay wincing when he says that. "What do you mean?"

Another wince before he waves his hand, and says, "Never mind."

"Hey, not fair. I've bared my soul to you, and you wave off my question."

"Leave it alone."

There's anger in his voice, so I don't push it, but I'm upset that apparently trust doesn't work both ways. Without another word, I grab a couple of boxes and head to my bedroom. I'm thankful now that I'm not much of a pack-rat and only accumulated necessities after Martin left me with nothing.

Jay walks in and starts helping. "I'm sorry," he whispers. "I really want to tell you, but I can't yet."

I stop working and turn to look at him. "That's all you had to say. I understand that better than anyone. Look how long it took me to tell you. And trust me when I say, you're the only one who knows the full detail. Plus, I still haven't scratched the surface of the mental toll it took on me. And not just the stuff Martin did and said."

"Then, let's both agree that once we each feel ready, we'll talk about these things."

"Agreed."

Before I realize what he's doing, Jay pulls me into his arms. My body's tight against his, and I start melting. He finishes me off with a kiss even hotter than the last one. There's a tenderness within his passion that sends me soaring into another dimension. When he slides his tongue in my mouth, my knees go weak, and I have to hold on tight to keep from hitting the floor.

"I love you," he whispers when he breaks the kiss.

"I love you, too." I'm not sure whether to be happy or petrified at how easy it was to say that. I'm definitely falling for him, but that fear is always there after what happened in my last relationship. Even though Jay couldn't be more opposite of Martin, I still feel like I need to protect myself.

Apparently, we're both energized by the power of us in that moment. We lose track of time and finish the rest of the packing in record speed. After we load all the boxes into my car and Jay's truck, I leave my key on the counter and head out. Now, it's just a matter of figuring out where I'm gonna live.

"Follow me," Jay says before he gets in his truck. I do as told with furrowed brows. He turns right out of the parking lot, and I'm right on his tail as curious as ever about what he's doing. It doesn't take me long to figure out he's headed to his house. Maybe he has some contacts that can find me temporary housing.

I pull next to him in his massive driveway.

I bet that's not all that's massive.

Tammy, you naughty girl.

Yeah so? I haven't had it in far too long.

Shut up.

I bet he's huge down there.

I snicker at the argument in my head. Jay walks over to my car, and my cheeks heat up. I pray he can't read my mind.

"Let's head inside and figure things out," Jay says.

"Is it okay if I bring Sadie?"

"Of course. Lorelei and Sookie will love her."

We head inside, and Jay puts the dogs in a stay. I slowly walk Sadie over. After a few minutes of sniffs, she lays down with the labs, and the three of them curl up together on the blanket. I remove Sadie's leash and join Jay in the living room.

"I think they'll be fine," he says, a twinkle in his eye.

"So, are we here because you have someone who can rent me a place?"

"No, silly. You're staying with me until you find something."

My heart leaps. "Look, I appreciate how you're always coming to my rescue, but I feel like I'm taking advantage."

"I promise, you aren't. I wouldn't have offered it if I didn't want you here."

Good, because I really want to be here. For the first time in a long time, being with someone, I mean truly being with them, doesn't send me into a panic. I'll never forget what he said about my scar.

Instead of saying that, I just say, "Well, then, I'll just say thank you. But please, at least let me pay some rent."

"I won't hear of it. I'm a stubborn asshole, so I promise, you won't win a battle with me," Jay teases.

"Fine, I surrender."

"That's my girl."

We're about to head outside when we hear a truck pull into the driveway. Jay looks out and sees Mel and Judd.

"Are you okay with them knowing?"

"Um, it depends what you mean."

"Well, we haven't really defined what we are past friends, so that's your call."

"Can we just tell them I had to leave my apartment, and you're helping me out temporarily?"

"Yeah, I mean, it's the truth anyway."

"Thanks."

I follow Jay to the door and we meet the lovebirds in the driveway.

"Well, well, well, what do we have here?" Mel teases when she sees me before she gives me a big hug.

"Unfortunately, I had to vacate my apartment. So, Jay's been kind enough to let me stay until I find something permanent."

"He's a good man," Mel says.

"That he is."

"We were just getting ready to unload Tammy's boxes," Jay says.

"Well, then, put us to work," Judd says.

With the four of us, it doesn't take long to get everything done. "Thanks so much, everyone. I really need to return the favor somehow," I say.

"Nonsense. We're friends," Mel says. "But hey, I have an idea. Do you like board games?" Mel asks me.

"Oh yeah. I used to play a lot before my divorce. I miss that." I sigh, remembering how much fun I used to have.

"How about dinner and a men versus women game of *Pictionary* tomorrow night? If that's okay with you, Jay, since it's your house," Mel says.

Jay looks at me, and I nod yes. Mel's eyebrows shoot up. She starts rocking back and forth. Judd puts a hand on her, and she calms down, but I know she's dying to ask something. Apparently, Jay notices, too.

"Okay, I know you wanna know something, so ask," Jay says to Mel.

"What's really going on here?"

Jay looks at me again. "Let's just say we're getting to know each other," I say.

"Fair enough, but I wanna be the first to know if anything changes," Mel commands with a wink.

"Yes, ma'am," Jay teases.

Judd and Mel hang out for a while. It feels good to just sit and laugh with people who actually like me. After they leave, it hits me how exhausted I am.

"I hate to cut the night short, but I really need to get some sleep," I say.

"I'm sure. It's definitely been quite the day. Good night, my butter-fly," Jay says.

"Your butterfly?"

"Yeah, your past was your cocoon, but look at you know. And I don't mean physically. Look how much fun you had tonight. No more people treating you like Martin did. Now, you're the most beautiful butterfly in the world."

I walk over to where Jay stands. I grab the back of his head and pull him to me. I crush my lips to his, savoring the taste of him, the way he feels, the way he smells. His arms wrap tightly around me as he deepens the kiss.

Without warning, I pull away. "Sweet dreams, Jay," I say with a wink as I walk into the guest bedroom and shut the door.

Chapter Seven

Jay

D id she really just do that? Turns out, that's quite the naughty girl that's been hiding in plain sight. And of course, she's left me unable to sleep. All I can think about is what it would feel like to be naked with her. To hold her close. To kiss her as I make love to her.

But I can't.

What? Where the fuck did that just come from?

But I know exactly where. How can I betray Dana?

****

I finally managed to get a little sleep, but it was anything but restful. I'm awakened by three furry faces breathing on me. As cute as they are, I know which face I really wanna see when I first wake up. Suddenly, my nose wakes up, and I inhale deeply. My house smells delicious. Forgetting for a moment that I'm not alone, I walk out to the kitchen in boxers and nothing else.

Tammy looks over, and I see her jaw drop. "Mmmm," she murmurs.

"I could say the same. Everything smells delicious."

"The least I could do is make you some breakfast. Have a seat." She puts a plate of eggs, bacon, and toast in front of me, along with a cup of black coffee.

I watch her fix her coffee with some *Splenda* and hazelnut flavored creamer she brought with her. I make a mental note to always have that on hand. Out of nowhere, I hear a trio of snoring from the living room. All three girls are curled up, sound asleep.

"How is that possible with the smell of bacon?"

"Well, before I cooked, I fed all three of them then took them out to run."

"Good plan!"

After we're done eating, I get up to carry the dishes over to the sink. Forgetting that I'm shirtless, I hear Tammy gasp when I get close. *Oh shit.*

"What happened?" She points at the scar on my abdomen. "I'm sorry. I shouldn't have blurted that out."

"No, it's okay. You've told me so much, and I've told you very little. So, I hope you're ready to learn something about me."

"I am, but please, only if you're ready."

"As ready as I'll ever be. And like when you told me, I just need you to let me tell the story."

"Of course."

I take her hand and walk her over to the couch. She sits sideways, and I face her. She keeps her hand in mine as I start.

"This is something that even Mel doesn't know, so please, I need you to keep this between us." She nods in agreement as she gives my hand a gentle squeeze. I now understand what made her so comfortable telling me. There's just something between us that's right.

"I was engaged. Her name was Dana. We had just set the date for our wedding when Dana got life-changing news. She had Type One Diabetes, which progressed into kidney failure at a young age. Her most recent lab work at the time showed that she had progressed to end-stage renal disease."

I have to pause. I can feel the tears threatening, and I will not let

Tammy see that. I don't want her thinking I'm not a real man. The moment passes, so I keep going.

"A kidney transplant would've been her best option, so I got tested. Miracle of miracles, I was a match. It took a little while for me to convince her to let me do this. I was healthy and there would be minimal risk for me to donate. Once I finally convinced her, we scheduled the surgery."

Tammy moves closer to me, and I can see the concern on her face. I'm having a hard time holding back my tears as I prepare for the hardest part of the story. "It's okay to let it all out," she whispers.

This woman is amazing.

"Everything went well. Well, at least we thought it had. I recovered fully in the normal amount of time for this type of procedure. Dana was responding well to the anti-rejection medications, but something changed. Her body rejected the kidney, and they weren't able to save her."

I'm no longer able to fight the tears and they stream down my cheeks. I hang my head in shame. But then, I feel a pair of soft hands on my face. Tammy gently lifts my head. "Never be ashamed to show your emotions."

"I don't want you to think less of me as a man."

"Oh, Jay, nothing could be further from the truth. I admire a man who's not afraid to show how he's feeling. Truly, if you didn't cry, I'd see you as cold and unfeeling. But, that's not you."

"Thank you for saying that." She wraps her arms around my neck and hugs me. I can't believe how much of a weight this has lifted off of me. I didn't realize just how much of a burden carrying this secret was for me. "Is there anything you wanna ask?"

"Is that why you've never been with anyone else?"

"Yeah. I mean I've had dates, one night stands, all that shit, but never anything more. I was starting to think I never would. But then, something incredible happened. Actually, someone incredible. And the night I realized how strong my feelings for you are, Dana came to me in a dream."

"Oh, wow. What happened?"

"She told me you were the one I'd been waiting for and not to mess it up."

"Wow."

"Yeah, but part of me feels like I'm betraying her."

"I can't imagine, so I won't offer advice. But if you feel the need to just remain friends like we've been, I understand."

"But, Tam, that's the thing. I wanna be with you."

"I know, and I wanna be with you too, but you need to be ready. And if you're not, we don't need to rush. But we should hurry down to the bar. We lost so much time yesterday, and there's a lot of work to do."

She just seems to know exactly what I need. We load all three dogs in the backseat of my truck and head to The Full Moon. As soon as we pull into the parking lot, and I see the big front window, my body catches on fire.

"Martin," Tammy whispers.

Spray painted in big bright red letters are the words *A big, fat pig works here.*

"If it was him, he's in deep shit."

"But how will you be able to prove it?"

"See the two new lights on either side of the door?"

"Yeah."

"They're also cameras covering the whole parking lot. I put them in so that in case anyone tries anything out here, we'd have proof. So, our first order of business is to call the police and review the footage. Then, we'll figure out what to do about the window."

"Well, whatever we do, it should come out of my salary."

"Absolutely not. Martin will be paying, or whoever did this. I promise you that."

"Okay."

As we walk inside, I notice Tammy's head down, staring at her feet, "Nope. Get that chin up. This is not your fault." She smiles, and my heart swells.

Suddenly, out of nowhere, Dana pops into my head. *I told you not to mess this up. The only way you'll betray me is to deny yourself, to deny this woman, the happiness you both deserve.*

And that quickly, she's gone again. Something just changed inside me, and it feels damn good. And then my brain takes off like the Concorde, and I hatch a plan that's going to sweep my butterfly off her beautiful feet.

Tammy sits down, again hanging her head and my heart breaks. I really need to help her get rid of this blaming herself for Martin's actions, but first I need to make sure it really was him. I dial the local police, and a little while later, two officers come in. We all head to my office, and as I suspected, Martin appears on video defacing the window.

"This clown have a name?" one of the officers asks.

"Martin Foster. He's my ex-husband. The vandalism is my fault."

"No, ma'am, it's not. It's his. Do you know where we can find him?"

"I'm sorry. I'm not sure where he lives now."

"It's okay. We'll find him. And he'll pay. We'll be in touch." The officers head out.

"I'm gonna run to the hardware store and grab some wood until we can get that window cleaned. Can you do me a favor and take inventory of all the glassware?"

"Sure thing. Do you have sheets? If not, I'm pretty good with Microsoft Excel, so I can make some."

"I haven't had a chance, so that would be great. There's a surprise upstairs for you. You'll know it when you see it."

I wait by the front door. I hear Tammy squeal when she sees a door with her name on it. I left the key in the lock for her. She screams when she sees the inside. She now has an L-shaped desk, a luxury leather chair complete with a massager, and a state of the art computer and printer. I also added several framed pictures of Sadie, Sookie, and Lorelei and finished the decorating off with a large framed painting of a butterfly.

"It's the most amazing thing I've ever seen!" she shouts down the steps.

"I'm glad you like it. Now get to work," I tease.

"Yes, sir," she says with a salute, and we both laugh.

By the time I get back, she has every different type of glass categorized and counted on her sheet. I knew I made the right choice promoting her. "Wow, you finished way more than I expected."

"I believe in earning my pay. I'm not at all what that asshat says I am. And thanks to you, I'm finally starting to believe that."

"That's my girl." *And oh, you have no idea how much you're my girl.* I cannot wait for tomorrow night. Especially since she has no idea what's coming.

"Earth to Jason, come in Jason."

Oops, she caught me daydreaming. "Sorry, spaced for a second. What's up?"

"What time are Mel and Judd coming? I need to make sure I have enough time to get dinner ready and I need to stop at the store."

"Mel said around five, so we'll probably head out soon. Now, I do need to ask because I wasn't sure earlier. Do you like your office?"

"Oh, ha, ha! I love it. Thank you so much."

"Only the best for my second in command."

Tammy finishes inventory of plates and silverware then we call it a day. "I'll put these all in my computer tomorrow. I'm going to build some formulas to keep track of things so that each time we do inventory, we'll be able to track changes."

"Perfect. But now, it's time to turn our focus to fun. If you're good in the store by yourself, I'll stay in the truck with the trio."

"Absolutely."

****

As I'm waiting for Tammy, I see someone approaching my truck. He holds his middle finger high in the air, pointing right at me. As he gets closer, I realize why. Fuckin' Martin. I grab my wallet and call one of the officers from earlier. While I'm waiting, it hits me. Shit. He came out of the store. He comes right to the window and flips me off again. I hear a sound from all three dogs I've never heard before.

They all stand there growling, the hair on their back standing straight up. Dogs are definitely good judges of character. They hit the nail on the head here. "Can I help you?"

"Nope, but *she's* gonna need help."

"What the fuck did you do this time?"

"You'll find out."

"You really are an asshole."

"Yeah, and you're a pig-lover. Oink oink oink."

I get out of the truck, and I'm about to deck him when someone grabs my arms. I turn and see Judd. "Whoever he is, he's not worth it, man," Judd says.

"Meet Tammy's ex."

"Oh. Well, then he's definitely not worth it. How could anyone leave a woman that amazing? I just don't understand what's wrong with some dudes."

"Yeah, me either. But their loss is our gain."

"Right. Now, sir, I strongly suggest you move along. There's no need to keep tormenting Tammy. And you won't be, at least for a while."

"Meaning what, asshole?"

I don't respond. Instead, I stand with Judd and watch as Martin's cuffed and put in the back of a police car. I know he won't do any time, but there's still some satisfaction seeing him in cuffs.

"Thanks, man. I was this close to hitting him," I say to Judd.

"I get the instinct. I can't tell you how many times I wanted to lay out Derek. Even more, I wanted to get Daniel in the worst way, after what he put Mel through at work."

"You weren't alone there."

"Dude," Judd says as he nods his head toward the store. I see Tammy heading toward us pushing a shopping cart with a couple of bags. Her head hangs, and I feel like someone punched me in the gut. Judd and I walk toward her. Judd takes the cart and walks to my truck.

"What did he say?"

"Who?"

"I know Martin was in the store. He decided it was a good idea to stop by the truck. I woulda decked him this time, but Judd saved me."

"The usual. I'm just so damn tired of it. Why can't he just leave me alone?"

"Might I give an opinion?" Judd asks when we reach him.

"Of course," Tammy says.

"He's regretting throwing you away. Look at how far you've come.

And now, he sees you healthy and in the company of a man like Jay. But he can't admit he made a mistake, so instead he's lashing out at you."

"That makes sense, but it's not right," Tammy says.

"Oh, I agree. I just want you to know that it's not you. Jay and I are two very lucky men to have found you and Mel."

Tammy's face lights up. "Thank you so much for saying that."

"I meant every word. Now, I need to grab a couple of things and get home before Mel kicks my butt. We'll see you tonight. Oh, and by the way, Jay has something to tell you."

"What's up?" Tammy says.

"I called the cops when I saw Martin coming toward my truck, so he's on his way to the police station."

A smile fills her beautiful face.

"Now, I'm especially looking forward to it," I say. I take the bags from Judd and put them in the truck. He takes the cart Tammy had and heads off to get whatever Mel needs. I knew she'd never show up empty-handed, even though Tammy told her she didn't need to bring anything but her appetite.

"So, what's for dinner? I'd like to help."

"I'm gonna do a taco bar. But with ground turkey."

"Oh, that sounds delicious."

****

We're just getting everything set up on the counter when the doorbell rings. "Come in," I call out.

The door swings open, and I see Daisy and Lily make a beeline for the other dogs. After a round of "singin,." they all settle down and crowd onto Lorelei and Sookie's blanket. We all can't help but laugh.

Mel walks into the kitchen and puts a cake carrier down. "Chocolate cake with mint buttercream icing."

"Oh wow, Mel, that sounds delicious," Tammy says.

"It is, especially when you eat it off the chest of a sexy cowboy!"

"Oh my god!"

"Pretty much what I was screaming." Mel smirks.

46

"Should we be worried?" I ask Judd when I see Mel and Tammy laughing together in the kitchen.

"I definitely am. If I know my girl, she's telling Tammy something dirty. That's what you get to look forward to."

"Tammy and I are just friends."

"Dude, seriously."

"Well, right now we are."

"That's more like it."

Chapter Eight

Tammy

After we finish eating, Mel helps me clean up while Jay and Judd set up the game table and chairs. Jay grabs his Pictionary game out the closet and sets the board up on the table. Two games later, after Mel and I mopped the floor up with the guys, we're sitting at the table enjoying coffee and a piece of the cake Mel baked.

A while later, all five dogs start stirring and line up in front of the sliding glass door. "I'm gonna take them all out back," Jay says.

"I'll join you," Judd adds.

"Me too," Mel chimes in. "You comin', Tammy?"

"Be right there. I wanna clean up the game first."

I sit down and start putting the game away. Before I do, I grab a piece of paper and one of the pencils and start drawing. I'm so lost in what I'm doing, I don't notice everyone come back inside. I feel Jay's presence between, and I hear him gasp.

"What's wrong?" I ask.

"Did you just draw that?"

"Oh, I was just doodling."

"Like hell. That's amazing."

Mel and Judd walk over to see what all the fuss is about. "Oh my god, it's Jay. I had no idea we had an artist among us," Mel says in a high-pitched voice.

"I'm hardly an artist."

"Uh, yeah, you are," Judd says.

"How long have you known you could do this?" Jay asks.

"The first art class I ever took was in middle school. My teacher was blown away," I say.

"How come you never pursued it?" Jay asks.

"Because it was a stupid waste of time," I say with a sigh.

"Ah, now I get it. You didn't feel that way, did you?" Jay asks.

"No," I say softly.

Mel sits down next to me and puts her hand on my arm. "Listen to me. I know what it's like to let a man's opinion make you feel less than. And I also know what it feels like to rid yourself of that and find a man who builds you up." She stops and looks at Judd, a twinkle in her pretty eyes. "You need to free yourself."

"Easier said than done."

"I know. But, I have an idea, if you're up for it."

"What?"

Mel takes a blank piece of paper and a pencil. She writes Martin and his negative comments on the paper. "Jay, can we borrow your fire pit?" Mel asks.

"Of course. Let's go," Jay says.

Mel hands me the piece of paper as the four of us walk outside. Jay ignites the flame, and we all stand around it.

"When you're ready, drop that sucker into the fire," Mel says.

I lean in toward the pit and hold the paper out. Mel gives me a reassuring squeeze on my shoulder as I drop the paper and watch it burn to nothing but ash.

"Now, how did that feel?" Mel asks.

"Good," I say.

"Uh-uh. I can see it on your face. It's more than just good. Go ahead, girl, and shout it out," Mel says.

I lift my head toward the sky and with all my might, I shout, "I'm finally fucking free, and it feels so damn good!"

"That's more like it, my friend," Mel says and gives me a hug then goes and stands with Judd.

Jay walks over, and apparently forgetting we have guests, drops a kiss on me like nothing I've ever felt. I vaguely recall hearing hoots and hollers from Mel and Judd, but all I really remember is the primal intensity of his lips on mine, his tongue aggressively exploring my mouth. He breaks the kiss, and I can barely remember where I am.

"Um, wow," is all Mel can manage to utter.

"Dude," Judd adds.

I'm still having trouble processing anything going on around me. "Um, yeah, well," Jay stammers.

"I think that's our cue to head home," Mel teases.

"Yeah, give the lovebirds some alone time," Judd adds.

Mel snorts loudly as she laughs, finally snapping me back to reality. The sensation of Jay's strong lips is still on mine ,and I want more. More than just a kiss. But I don't say anything. My cheeks feel like they're on fire. Not to mention some other parts of my body.

We gather up the dogs and head inside. I put some leftovers in containers and bag them up for Mel and Judd. She leaves some cake. "Remember what I said about the icing," Mel says with a wink, and I laugh.

We walk them out and wave until they're out of the driveway. We walk back inside and sit down next to each other on the couch.

"I'm so sorry for doing that in front of them," Jay says.

"It's okay. I think they were already suspecting things were moving toward the possibility of being more than friends," I say.

"I think so, too. Judd said as much when I saw him at the store earlier. And on that topic, I think at some point we need to talk about it. But not tonight."

"Yes, I'm exhausted after everything that happened today."

"Me too. Let me finish cleaning up. You've already done so much."

"But I wanna help."

"Okay. Tell ya what. You take the dogs out to do their last business for the night while I take care of this."

"Works for me!"

After I get back inside, Jay locks up, sets the alarm, and we both head upstairs to our bedrooms.

****

The next morning after breakfast, we head down to the bar to do some more inventory. Once we're done, I head up to my office to start entering the numbers into my computer and get the sheets set up to make future counting more streamlined. I love this nerdy math stuff. I'm a weird combination of nerdy and artistic. I've never really been one who liked to conform, but I let Martin make me. With Jay, I can be myself, and he still likes me.

As I'm finishing up, Jay appears in my doorway. "I love the look on your face when you get lost in your work."

As I always do when he flatters me, I blush. "Thanks."

"So, how much do you have left?"

"I'm on the last page. Should take me another ten minutes."

"Mind if I just hang out? Once you're done, I have a surprise for ya."

"You wanna watch me work?" I blush harder.

"Yeah. Unless that makes you uncomfortable."

"Nah, after all, you're my boss, so it's your right to supervise me."

"True, but that's not why I'm doin' it. I just like looking at you."

Is it possible to blush even more? My face is on fire as I finish up. My typing skills take a nosedive with his eyes on me. But, and I'd never tell him this, there's something exciting about him gazing at me. I can't believe I feel that way. I never would have before. He's definitely helped me find a confidence that I didn't know was buried in my soul.

"All done," I say as I start shutting my computer down.

"Great. Let's go. I already have everything we need in the truck."

"What about the dogs?"

"They're at Mel and Judd's house for the night."

"When exactly did you do all this?"

"You were up here working away, so I snuck out."

I smile as butterflies fill my stomach. What on earth could he have in store for me? Again, I struggle between excitement and fear. But one thing I know for sure, with Jay I'm always safe. He'd never hurt me.

We get into Jay's truck, and he heads out of the parking lot. He won't give me so much as a hint where we're going. Nothing looks familiar in this direction, and I'm intrigued. After a while, he pulls into a small parking lot. Other than a couple of small, round picnic tables, there's nothing but wildflowers as far as the eye can see.

Jay walks around to my door, opens it, and holds out his hand. "Our destination, my lady."

I get out of the truck and wait while Jay grabs a blanket, picnic basket, and guitar case out of the back seat.

"Ah, the return of the famous guitar."

"Hey, you gotta stick with what works," he teases.

"I see that. I can't wait to hear more."

We walk to one of the tables and sit down. Jay lays the blanket on the ground, then unpacks the picnic basket on the table. "Chicken salad sandwiches and a fresh fruit salad for your dining pleasure. I also have a variety of low sugar drinks."

"Wow, everything looks delicious." *But not nearly as delicious as you.*

Naughty girl.

Yeah so?

I'm horny. And he's hot.

Why am I always arguing with myself? Good lord.

After we eat, Jay puts all the trash into the basket. He takes my hand and leads me to the blanket. "Please come sit with me," he says. There's a sultriness to his voice tonight, and I'm not gonna lie, it sets my insides on fire. I watch as he takes the guitar out of the case. He starts strumming, and I recognize the song right away.

"How did you know I was a fan of Brett Eldredge?"

"I saw the CDs when we were packing up your apartment. Now lie back and listen, sweetie."

I lay back and close my eyes as Jay sings Brett's song *The Long Way*. I'm as blown away at his talent as I was the first time he sang. More than that, I feel more of the wall around my heart crumbling away. I wiggle closer to him and lay my head on his chest, listening to his heart beat as he sings to me. He finishes the song, and I feel his arms tighten around me.

"I'm in love with you," he whispers in my ear.

My eyes shoot open, but I don't move my head. It feels so right to lie in his arms that I never want to stop. I never want to be anywhere else. "I'm in love with you, too," I say.

He gently rolls me onto my back and kisses me. The kiss is a magical combination of passion, desire, love, and tenderness. The way he slowly teases me with his tongue drives me wild, and I growl into his mouth. The sound awakens something in him, and he deepens the kiss. I'm on the verge of losing all control. And for the first time in my life, I'm not afraid.

Chapter Nine

Jay

H oly shit. That's the hottest kiss I've ever shared with a woman. I get up and hold out my hands to help Tammy up.

"Please dance with me," I say. I grab my cell, open *Spotify*, and pull up the playlist I made just for tonight, filled with love songs from the eighties. It feels like being back in high school. I take Tammy into my arms, pulling her tight against me. I hear her sigh softly as she lays her head on my shoulder. Her hair smells like coconut, and I inhale deeply, enjoying everything about this woman.

"Mmmm, Jay," she murmurs. All I can think about is how she would feel, how she would sound, how she would look naked in my bed as we made love. I've never wanted anyone as much as I want her now. I know she's too private to do anything out in the open, but I'm hoping when we get home, she'll be ready to take that step.

"Can we go?" she asks.

"Go home?"

"Yeah."

"Is everything okay?"

"Oh yes."

"Then why the rush to go home?"

She looks at her feet, cheeks aflame, and I have a feeling I know what she's thinking. But I'm not letting her off the hook. I want her to feel safe enough to tell me what she wants. Besides, there's little that turns me on more than a woman who knows what she wants sexually and isn't afraid to say it.

"Oh, never mind."

"Uh uh. You're gonna tell me. I know there's something you want. Don't be afraid to ask."

"But men don't like that."

"Don't like what?"

"Pushy broads."

"Well, I don't even need to ask who said that. Let me tell you somethin'. I love a woman who's assertive and confident enough to tell me what she wants. That's such a turn on. I've never been afraid of strong women. Any man who has his own shortcomings that he's trying to compensate for."

"Shortcomings is an understatement. Mr. Zippy-Dick left a lot to be desired, if you know what I mean."

I can't help but laugh, and Tammy joins me. "Now, my butterfly, please tell me why you wanna go home."

"Okay. And please know this is very scary for me to do."

"I understand."

"Jay, I want to be with you. Really be with you. I-I-I want you to make love to me."

"Oh, baby, there's nothing I want more." I race over and grab all our stuff. We practically run back to my truck like two horny teenagers. I race home and after we're parked in the driveway, I drop everything in the kitchen.

We fly upstairs to my bedroom, and I escort her inside. "Baby, are you sure you still want this? I don't want you to feel any pressure."

"I've never wanted anything more. Please, Jay, I have to be naked with you. Now."

"Wow. It's like something's awakened inside you."

"Yeah, and it's all thanks to you and how you've treated me. But now, there's only one thing I want inside me." She gently drags her hand over the outside of my jeans, and my dick responds.

"Please, guide me so this is comfortable for you."

"I used to be so scared of anyone seeing me because of the scar, but after you saw it and after what you said, I'm not."

"Then tell me what you want me to do. I want this to be exactly what you want it to be."

"Oh Jay," she whispers as she kicks off her sneakers and slides her socks off. Suddenly, a switch flips and she stands in front of me, her hands on her hips.

"Please, Mr. Sexy, undress me. Slowly. I want you to savor every inch of my skin."

Holy fuck. Who is this woman? My beautiful butterfly is finally spreading her wings. And now, all I can think about is spreading her beautiful legs. I lift her shirt over her head and toss it aside. I gently glide my finger up her scar, and she shivers, moaning softly. Her bra follows and my god, she's stunning.

I drop to my knees and unfasten her jeans, I slowly slide them down her body. She holds onto my shoulders as she steps out of them. The scent of her desire fills the room and my dick hardens more. I hook my thumbs under her panties and slide them off. I run my hands down her cute little bottom and all the way down her legs,and she shivers harder. I love the effect my touch has on this beauty.

I'm in awe as I gaze up at the goddess standing before me in all her naked glory.

"I want you to touch me," she says.

"Where?"

"Between my legs."

I tease the insides of her thighs.

"Not there."

"Then be more specific," I say with a wink.

"Please touch my pussy," she begs. "I wanna feel your tongue."

Damn. She's an animal, and I love it. I swipe my tongue inside her folds, stopping to tease her clit. She latches her hands on my shoulders as her legs start shaking. Her moans intensify at the same pace as my tongue until she explodes around me. Fuck, she tastes so damn sweet.

"Mmm, so good, Jay. Oh, baby." She saunters over to the bed, an extra sway in her sexy little ass, and lays down. I watch as she props herself up on the pillow and licks her lips. "Now, strip for me. Slowly. And I better enjoy it."

I'm not the best dancer, but hours upon hours of sitting through *Dancing with the Stars* with Mel taught me a few moves. I put some gyration in my hips as I strip for her. She hoots and hollers as more and more of my skin's exposed. Of course, I save my underwear for last. When I finally strip my briefs off, I don't take my eyes off her face. Her eyes go wide as she smiles from ear to ear.

A wolf whistle escapes her lips as she wags her finger. I walk to the bed. "Where do you want me?"

"On your back. There's something I've always wanted to try, but for some reason, men don't like it."

"Well, now I'm intrigued. What might that be?"

"I've always wanted to be on top."

"Um, who told you men don't like that? Wait, never mind. Trust me, most men do."

"Then slide to the center of the bed. I'm gonna take you on the ride of your life, baby," she says, her voice so sultry I almost shoot early.

She straddles me, hovering over my dick. Grabbing me with one of her soft, little hands, she positions my dick at her opening and very slowly slides down until I'm all the way inside her. Fuck, she feels like heaven. She locks eyes with me, leans forward, and starts to slide her slick pussy up and down my shaft.

"No, baby, not like that. I wanna see you. All of you." I grab her hips to brace her. "Now, sit up straight.'"

She does as she's told and again starts sliding up and down my dick. I bend my knees to give her somewhere to lean if she needs it. That frees my hands to explore her soft body. I tease her clit with my thumb as I meet her rhythm with thrusts of my own. She emits primal growls as she moves closer to another explosion. I'm not too far away myself. Nothing would be more amazing than to come together. To know that we truly are one.

"I love you so fucking much!" I scream out as I fill her with my cum. That sends her over the edge, and she explodes. This orgasm is so much more intense than her first one, and I can feel her quaking around me. She can't seem to stop as she angles herself so her clit rubs against my dick. She screams as she comes again before flopping down on top of me.

I hold her close as her breathing finally starts to return to normal. She can barely speak as I help her lay next to me. I pull her close, and she lays her head on my chest.

"Wow. I never knew it could feel like that. That was by far the most incredible sex I've ever had. I love you, Jay."

I run my fingers through her soaking wet hair, and I can feel myself getting horny again. "Oh baby, I hope you're not spent. I need you again."

"Please, I want you again, too. But this time, I want you on top of me. I need that. I wish I could explain it."

"You don't need to. I know exactly what you mean. Now, get ready for the most tender lovemaking you've ever experienced. And be ready, because I intend to make it last a long, long time."

We spend the next hour holding each other, eyes locked, breathing in perfect sync as we make love. She moves beneath me, and it feels so good. The painstakingly slow build to our crescendo leads to the most melodious duet of moans I've ever heard. I empty inside her, and after I move next to her, I send her over the edge by licking her clit. The taste of both of us fills my tongue, and it's delicious.

I pull the covers over us, turn the lights off, and within seconds, I hear the softest little snores. I gently kiss the top of her head, drifting off to sleep to the rhythm of her breathing.

****

"Good morning, gorgeous," I say when I feel Tammy stir awake. She stretches her arms out and sighs, as her eyes slowly open.

"Mmmm, good morning," she responds, her eyes fluttering. Damn, she's so cute.

"How 'bout a shower my love?"

"You can go first if you'd like."

"Actually, I thought we'd go together."

"What! I can't do that."

"Why?"

"Because you'll see me."

"I saw you last night."

"Yeah, but that was the heat of the moment. This is different."

"No, sweetie, it's not. You're still the same beautiful woman that I made love with last night. Now, please give me the chance to pamper you."

"I guess. But if I change my mind, will you let me finish the shower alone?"

"Deal."

"Thanks for putting up with all my ridiculous hang-ups."

"Nothing ridiculous about it. Look how far you've come already. We'll get rid of those insecurities once and for all. It'll just take time."

Tammy looks at me and nods. I take her hand, and we walk to the bathroom together. I go to the sink to brush my teeth. She stands next to me and starts doing the same. She looks so serious that it's time to lighten the mood. I start making faces at her in the mirror. She gives me a light elbow in the side, which only spurs me on. I up my face-game, and next thing I know, there's toothpaste all over the mirror.

"You dick! Now I have to clean your mirror."

"In all fairness, I should be the one to clean it, since I made you spit."

"Yeah, you should."

After I do a quick wipe of the mirror, I open the doors to my shower stall and turn the water on to let it warm up. I hold Tammy's arm as she steps in and position her under the removable shower head. I rinse her from head to toe and grab the puff she brought.

I grab her bottle of *Bath & Body Works* shower gel and look at the label. Freesia. I squirt some onto the puff, and the scent is intoxicating. I start lathering her body. She closes her eyes. The look of bliss on her face rivals the one I saw in bed last night. After rinsing her, I shampoo and condition her hair. The scent of strawberries is now mixed with the freesia, and I can barely control myself.

When she's done, I ask, "Did you enjoy that?"

"Ahh, yes, so relaxing. My turn now."

The devilish look in her pretty green eyes makes my knees go weak. *Bath & Body Works* is apparently the retailer of choice, as I use the Coffee and Whiskey gel. She skips the washcloth and instead uses her hands. Her soft skin feels so good running all over my skin, but when she gets to *that* area, holy shit!

She grabs my shampoo and starts washing my hair. With her height, she has no issue reaching the top of my head. Her medium length nails feel so good as she scrubs my scalp, and for the second time, I nearly go down. She finishes rinsing me and throws her arms around my neck.

"Thank you for giving me the courage to do this. I've never showered with anyone before, and it was amazing,"

"I'm honored to be your first." She looks at me and smiles. My heart flutters, and for a brief moment, I panic at the hold this woman has on me. But I'll never tell her that.

Chapter Ten

Tammy

After breakfast, we head over to Judd and Mel's house to pick up the dogs. I know if Mel gets me alone, she's gonna know what happened last night. Part of me wants to tell her, but part of me feels like I shouldn't since she and Jay are such good friends. No need to focus on that now. I switch my brain back to last night. And oh my heavens, what a night it was.

We pull into the driveway and Mel comes bouncing outside. "Judd's in the backyard," she says to Jay.

"Okay, I can take a hint," he teases and heads out back.

Mel grabs my hand and after nearly pulling my arm off its socket, she drags me inside. We sit down across from each other at the kitchen table. "Every last little detail, woman."

"What do you mean?"

"Oh no, no, no. You can't pull that off. I see the difference in you two this morning. It happened didn't it?"

I'm not giving in that easily. "What happened?"

"Tammy Foster!" I know damn well you two had sex."

Damn, she's good. I turn beet red and drop my head. "Yeah. But I don't feel right talking about it. He's your friend."

"I appreciate that, but I'm also a horny little gossip. Now, no need to describe his nakedness or anything, but please. Give me something. I need the gossip."

I can't help but laugh at her desperation. I've never had a female friend like her, and I never realized what I was missing. "He's so tender and loving. That rough and tough exterior hides quite the teddy bear."

Mel sits with her elbows on the table, head resting on her palms. "Awww. I love that. He truly is a gentle giant. I'm so happy you two found each other. I was starting to wonder if he'd ever let himself love."

There's so much I wish I could say, but it's not mine to tell. "I wasn't sure I would. Martin had me feeling so terrible about myself with all the things he said. But Jay wouldn't let that fly. He made it so easy to trust him. To open up to him. That was the turning point for us."

Tears filling her eyes, Mel gets up and gives me a big hug. "Thank you for loving my friend."

"My pleasure," I say with a wink.

"You know, they've been watching us the whole time. I bet it's killing them that they don't know what we're talking about."

"Let them wonder. I'll never tell!"

"That's my girl," Mel teases. "How about we join them, just to to torture them a bit? And right before I open the sliding glass door, think of the funniest thing you ever heard. I want them dying to know what's so funny."

"You're a meanie," I tease.

"Damn right!"

I recall a scene from the movie *Nothing to Lose* where Tim Robbins' character has a tarantula crawling on his head. He does the most hilarious dance trying to get it off, complete with setting his pants on fire. We're both laughing hysterically as Mel opens the back door, and we join the guys.

"This does not bode well for us," Judd says.

"I know what you mean. Mel's taking my sweet girl to the dark side."

"Hey," Mel says, hands firmly planted on her hips.

"Um, does that mean you think I don't have my own brain either?" I ask. I thought it was only my ex-husband who felt that way.

Jay gets up and walks over to me. "Oh, sweetie, I'm so sorry. Not at all what I meant. I was just teasing. I told you before how intelligent and strong-willed I think you are."

"Thanks," I whisper. "That jerk still gets in my head sometimes. I promise, I'm working on it."

"I know you are." Jay gives me a big hug, and every inch of my skin tingles at his touch.

Mel walks over and takes my hand. "Come take a walk with me."

We head down to the far corner of Mel and Judd's back yard. "I know exactly how you feel. I let Derek have a hold on me for way too long. I've seen a change for the positive in you. Just keep going that way. You will slip from time to time, I still do. Just work past it and keep moving forward."

"I really am trying."

"I can see that. And especially take this piece of advice. Whenever you start feeling that way, tell Jay. You know he'll help. The love I see in his eyes when he looks at you is like nothing I've ever seen from him. He'll be your strength when you need it. And you can do the same for him."

"Have you had to help Judd in that way?"

"I have. When Abby came back, after I got over the shock of seeing them together, a night I know you remember well, we talked. Seeing her brought up nothing but painful reminders from his past."

I nod, thinking about Dana. I can't imagine how much pain that caused, still causes, him. I need him to know that I'm there whenever he needs or wants to talk about it. "Thanks, Mel. I needed to hear that."

"I think we need a standing girl date. A time for us to go out, enjoy a meal, chat, maybe some retail therapy," Mel says.

"That sounds like fun, but don't you already have that with Lexi?"

"Not so much anymore. I mean, we'll always be friends, but our lives have gone in different directions. And since we sold the house next door to Damien, we don't see them as much."

"I'm sorry."

"It's okay. Life goes on. And I'm so excited to see you helping Jay do just that. But I'm also glad to see you this happy. I always felt like something was holding you back."

"Oh, trust me, it was."

"Tell me sometime?"

"I'll have to say maybe for now. It's not easy for me to talk about, but I did finally find the courage to tell Jay. And that's when things turned a corner for us."

That earns me another big hug. It's so nice to have a friend again after Martin made sure mine all turned on me. "So, when's our first girl's date? I love the idea of that. I used to have a group of friends, but when Martin left, they went with him."

"That sucks. Women can be such jerks. That's why I'm glad I found you. I've been feeling a bit down, and getting to know you has helped. I feel like we have a lot in common,"

"Me too. I forgot what I was missing out on. And hey, I could maybe use some help."

"Oh yeah, with what?"

"I have no idea how to buy clothes."

"Well, you've come to the right place. How about Friday night?"

"Count me in!"

"Yay! Let's go join the boys and fill them in. Ready to see them start sweating?"

I laugh out loud and say, "Damn right."

Mel and I walk arm in arm back to the table where the guys are just staring at us. It's been a long time since I've felt normal. It almost makes me forget everything I've been through, something I need once in a while.

The guys just stare as we return. I give Mel a side glance and she's trying her hardest not to laugh. I'm fighting too, and I feel myself losing. I get a picture in my head of the guys sitting here, sweat dripping off their brow, and that sends me over the edge. I lose control and find myself doubled over in laughter. That's all it takes and Mel does the same.

"What the hell is with you two?" Judd teases.

"Wouldn't you like to know?" I shoot back at him.

"Now *that's* my girl," Mel says, laughing.

"Rubbing off on my sweet girl, huh, Mel?" Jay adds.

Mel responds with a loud raspberry, and we all laugh. Each moment like this takes me one step further away from my past, and I can't put into words just how freeing it is.

****

Friday night rolls around and, as promised, Mel and Judd pull into Jay's driveway at five. They have her car tonight, since we're headed out. Somehow, Jay talked Judd into helping him with some stuff down at the bar. Though, I suspect they will mostly drink beer and shoot the shit. Probably about me and Mel.

"You boys have fun, and behave yourselves tonight," Mel teases.

"Um, I could say the same to you two ladies," Jay says.

Mel and I wink, and we head out.

"Where we headed?" I ask.

"I thought we'd work up an appetite at *Old Navy*. Gotta get you in some tighter jeans."

"Okay, but not too tight. I'd be embarrassed."

"How about like I wear them?"

"That's perfect. I have no idea what size or anything. I know these are too big, but, well, they just are."

"Hey, you can talk to me."

"I know."

I look over, and she smiles. Like Jay, she naturally makes you feel comfortable, and I'm not scared to tell her what I told Jay.

We get to the store and Mel parks. Once we're inside, she beelines right for the jeans and just starts grabbing stuff. She moves so fast, my head is spinning. I just watch her, trusting that she knows what she's doing, and she'll give me some tips along the way.

"To the dressing room, my friend," she says.

"I hate this part."

"I promise, it'll be painless."

"I trust you, so it better be!"

"Start with these." She hands me two pairs of jeans in two different sizes.

I try the larger size first, but they're still too loose. The next one down is better, but I think I could even go one more. And that feels amazing. It's been so long since I've had clothes that fit. Most don't because they are too big. I come out so Mel can see.

"I think one more size down," I say.

"I agree." She hands me one more pair, and I go back in.

This time, the first is perfect. I look in the mirror, and I can't believe that's me. I suddenly start feeling shy. "Mel, can you come in? I'm afraid to come out."

She comes in and whistles. "Damn, girl, you look amazing. Jay's gonna be drooling. These are the ones. Now, it's time to find some shirts."

Hurricane Melissa gains wind speed, and I have a pile of shirts to try on. We find the perfect size, and I'm really excited at how good I feel. Once we decide on what I'm gonna buy, Mel puts ten pairs of jeans and ten shirts in my cart.

"Now to bring Jay to his knees!"

"What do you mean?"

"Lingerie."

I turn beet red, especially when my mind wanders back to the night we had sex. Oh my god, that night! "I love that idea! Let's knock his socks off."

"That's my girl!"

We grab several sets of matching lace bras and panties and put them in the cart. We head up front, and I pay for all my stuff. "Thank you so much for this. You have no idea how much I needed it. And not just the clothes."

"I had a blast. But now I'm starving. Let's go find somewhere to eat. Are you hungry?"

"Oh no. I'm never hungry," I say, choking back tears.

"Hey, what's wrong?"

I wave my hand. "Oh nothing, let's just head to dinner like you said."

"Okay, but, woman, you are gonna talk to me."

I nod slightly, but I don't say anything. I guess I do owe her somewhat of an explanation after that freak-out. I just hope she'll still wanna be friends. And cue yet another internal argument.

Of course she will. Jay didn't run the hills, Mel won't either. She's been through her own stuff, so she'll understand.

No she won't.

Yes she will.

Wanna bet?

You'll remind her too much of her past, and she'll run.

Oh, shut up.

Mel pulls into the parking lot at the New Holland Family Restaurant. "How's this?"

"One of my favorites."

We head inside, and Mel asks for her favorite table in the back corner so we can talk. Our waiter, Todd, stops to take our order.

"Unsweetened iced tea, please" I say.

"And what would you like to eat?"

"I would like the broiled crab cakes with a baked sweet potato and coleslaw.

"And for you?" Todd asks Mel.

"I'll have the same as my friend."

"You ladies are making it easy on me," Todd says.

"We aim to please," Mel says.

"I bet you do," Todd says. He immediately turns red. "I'll, uh, put this right in for you." He hurries off to the kitchen.

"I feel like I owe you a bit of an explanation," I say.

"Please don't feel that way. But I'm willing to listen if you'd like to talk."

"Okay. I've already told all of this to Jay. It was the first time I'd told anyone. He made it so easy to trust him, to feel comfortable around him."

"I know what you mean. We hadn't been friends for that long when Derek left me. Nobody was there for me quite like Jay. I always wished I'd had a brother instead of my lousy sister, and Jay filled that void for me."

"I get it. I would have been happy with anyone. My parents had me, and that was it. Then, at eighteen, as soon as I was done high school, they informed me they'd done their job, and I was out. I owe Nick so much. He took a chance on me, hired me, and gave me a room to live in until I could afford an apartment."

"Wow. That's awful. I hope they were at least there for you when you went through things with Martin."

"Nope. They moved and didn't tell me where. I have no idea where to start if I wanted to find them. Which, quite honestly, I don't. That part, I haven't told Jay. He only knows about the shit with Martin,"

"Can I ask why the marriage failed?"

"In a nutshell, because Martin is a piece of garbage. And when I finish telling you this, I think you'll agree." I keep my eyes on Mel's face as I fill her in on my medical issues leading up to the divorce. By the time I say, "He served me with papers during my second hospital stay," tears are sliding down Mel's cheeks.

She grabs my hand and gently squeezes. "Oh, Tammy, I don't even know what to say. And yes, I completely agree with your assessment. Please know that none of the bad stuff he ever said is true. Judd and I adore you. And then there's Jay. I've never seen him feel this way about anyone. He's definitely in love with you."

"It took a while for me to let him in, but I'm so in love with him."

"And now, I have a game night partner!"

"That's the best part," I say, and we both laugh.

Todd brings our food and after we finish and pay the check, we head outside. We're about to get in Mel's car when my cell rings. Jay.

"Hello."

"Heyyyyy Tammyyyyy. Yous twos needs to comes to the, um, the, you know," Jay says. I put the phone on speaker.

"You mean the bar?"

"Yeppers. The bawr. Mes and Judds we needs you twos. Pweases."

Mel slaps her hand over her mouth in an attempt to stifle her laughter. "What the heck is wrong with you?" I tease.

"Lots and lots and lots of beers. So, so, so, so many beers. Yummy, yummy beers."

"We're on our way." I quickly disconnect, and we both lose it.

"I can only imagine what we're gonna find," Mel says.

"I'm not sure I wanna."

After we park, we head inside and both of us stop dead in our tracks. Jay and Judd are standing on stage, microphone in hand, screaming what sounds like a mixed up medley of Luke Bryan songs at the top of their lungs. And let's just say the barley and hops has made them the worst singers ever!

Jay looks over and apparently notices us. He grabs Judd's shoulder and shakes it. "Duuuuude. We gots groupies. And theys hotties. Wowie! Pwetty girlies." That's the last thing we hear before a thud when Jay goes on his ass.

"Melly, you so pwetty. Me lovie you," Judd says, slurring his words like crazy. Thud number two.

Now, both of these idiots are sitting on the stage, laughing their asses off.

"How are we gonna get them in your car and Jay's truck?" I ask.

"We're gonna need reinforcements. Hang tight." Mel walks up front and grabs her phone. After a couple of quick calls, we sit and wait. A little while later, Mikael comes in with another guy.

"Tammy, you already know Mikael. The man with him is Johnny. His wife is Eden, the owner of Garden of Eden."

"Oh wow, I love the food there," I say.

Johnny smiles, and says, "Thank you. I'll be sure to tell Eden."

"So, Mel, what'd you need our help with?" Mikael asks.

Mel points at the stage, and we watch as Mikael and Johnny double over in laughter.

"No way we'd be able to get them out to the parking lot and into the vehicles," I say.

Mikael and I get on each side of Jay while Mel and Johnny do the same with Judd. We guide them to the vehicles, and once they're secure, I run back and lock up the bar. Mikael is gonna follow me, and Johnny is gonna follow Mel to help get the guys inside.

"Thanks for a fun night," I say to Mel.

"I'll call tomorrow, and we can compare notes on whose man feels worse."

We all laugh and head home. Jay's sound asleep by the time I pull into the driveway. It takes Mikael, and I a few minutes to wake him enough to get him inside.

"Where should I deposit him?" Mikael says.

"I'll pull out the sleeper sofa, so we don't have to drag him upstairs."

Once we get Jay all settled on the bed, I walk Mikel to the door. "Thanks for helping me tonight."

"I'm always up for helping a damsel in distress," he teases.

"You're such a cinnamon roll," I say, thinking about my favorite type of romance novel hero.

"Hannah said the same thing to me before. You ladies and your codes." He laughs and shakes his head.

Once he's outside, I take the three dogs out for a last bathroom break. I get Jay's boots and socks off, but he's out cold and a dead weight, so I can't get any more clothes off. I get myself ready and curl up next to him, falling asleep to the sound of his heartbeat.

Chapter Eleven

Jay

"What the hell am I doing here?" I mutter when I realize I'm on the couch-bed. "And why the fuck is my head pounding?"

I stumble to the kitchen and see a note on the table.

Jay-

Down at the bar cleaning up after the cowboy sing-off. Dogs are fed and walked. Didn't know if you'd want breakfast so I just grabbed oatmeal before I left. See you later.

Love, Tammy

And now I'm even more confused. Plus, I keep getting this weird feeling that Mikael from the local pet shop was in my house. Am I finally losing my mind?

I trudge upstairs, and after a very unpleasant removal of stomach contents, I get in the shower. I'm feeling a little better, but not even close to being ready for food of any kind. I lie down and am awakened about an hour later by three, cold, wet noses. After I take them out for a quick potty, I head down to the bar.

When I get inside, the bar area is spotless, so whatever mess there was, Tammy did a great job. I see the light on in her office, so I head up.

"Wasn't sure I'd see you here today," she says.

"I'm surprised myself. Can you fill me in on what happened?"

"It will be my pleasure." A huge smile fills her face.

This does not bode well for me. She takes a deep breath, exhales and starts the sordid tale of *The Night Jay and Judd were Idiots*. By the time she's done, all I can do is stare at my feet. But at least I now know why I kept getting that feeling of seeing Mikael. Then, I remember something even worse, and I hope she doesn't.

She does...

"Oh and by the way, I have the entire extravaganza on video."

Damn security cameras. "Well, all I can say is I'm sorry."

"No need to be. Everyone needs a night like that sometimes."

"Did you and Mel have fun?"

"We sure did. She helped me pick out a bunch of new clothes. I have to run to her house later and get them. With everything that happened with you and Judd, I forgot to get my bags out of her car."

"Well, thank you for taking care of me, and for the immaculate clean-up you did downstairs."

"No problem at all, my love."

"I'm finally starting to feel like I could eat something."

"How about I run down to Garden of Eden and grab lunch? Can you handle a turkey sandwich?"

"That sounds great. I'll be in my office trying to get some work done while you're gone."

"Be back soon. Oh, and by the way, I had fun driving your truck!" She laughs as she bounces out the door.

I walk up to my office and start packing some of the supplies I ordered. I open one of the cabinets on the side wall, and I see a leather case. It looks like an art portfolio. Nick must have left it behind. I open it to see if it's something he might want, and I'm blown away at what I find.

Tammy's name is written in silver ink on the inside and there's a pile of her artwork. Everything from people to animals to landscapes. And every single piece is stunning. I wonder why Nick had it. I close it up and lay it on my desk.

I hear Tammy come back with lunch. She comes upstairs with a bag and puts it down. Her eyes go wide when she sees what's on my desk.

"Where did that come from?"

"I found it in a cabinet. How come Nick had it?"

"Well, Martin threatened to throw it out if I didn't stop wasting my time doodling. So, I brought it here and asked Nick to hold on to it. I forgot all about it. I can't believe he kept it."

"I wasn't trying to invade your privacy, but I looked inside to see if it was anything Nick might want. Babe, these drawings are stunning. You really should pursue this."

"It's too late."

"Why?"

"I'm old. What would I do in art school with a bunch of twenty-somethings?"

"First, you aren't old. We've just been alive longer. And you have life experiences those kids don't. Look, I'm not gonna push, but please, promise me you'll think about it."

"I promise."

After we finish lunch, Tammy cleans up. "I'm gonna head off to my office. Now that I have all of the inventory logged, I wanna see where we have shortages and place some orders. Do you want to approve everything before I do it?"

"Nope. I trust you."

She smiles. "Thanks. I'm still trying to adjust to feeling good about myself, so please keep being patient with me."

"You'll always be able to count on me, Butterfly."

I watch her walk out, and damn, I can't see that cute little bottom enough. Luckily, she's more focused than I am. She spends the rest of the afternoon getting everything we need ordered while I spend it fantasizing about her naked body. Hey, I'm a guy, what can I say?

****

I can't believe we're only one short week away from the grand re-opening. Tammy's been working so hard that I want to treat her to a weekend away. Of course, she tries to downplay her contributions.

"It's my job. It's what I'm paid to do."

"True, but you've gone above and beyond my expectations without being asked. And that matters. And to say thank you, I'm taking you away this weekend. Where we go is up to you."

"Wait, really? I actually get to go on a trip? I-I-I've never been welcome before."

"Okay, I'm gonna bite my tongue and just focus on us. So, where have you always wanted to go."

"Well, there is one place and the good news is, it's close."

"Oh yeah, where?"

"Atlantic City. I love the beach plus I kinda always wanted to see the inside of a casino."

"Well, there are plenty of choices. Do you know which one?"

"Whatever has the lowest price rooms."

"Nope. No way. Uh uh. I wanna take you exactly where you want. And I plan on spoiling you."

"But I don't deserve that."

"The hell you don't. Now tell me, woman."

"Okay. I really wanna stay at The Hard Rock."

"I was hoping that's the one you would pick. I've always wanted to see it, too. I'm curious, what games do you wanna try?"

"Well, years back, still in high school, I was home sick. I was flipping channels and *ESPN* was showing the World Series of Poker. I was intrigued, so I put it on. I was amazed at how high the pots were getting, Phil Hellmuth ended up winning, and I was hooked. I've played some free online sites, but never anything else."

"How've you done?"

"I can hold my own, but it might be different in person. I have no idea if I have a good poker face."

I grab my cell and dial Mel's number. "Hey, you and Judd free tonight?"

"Sadly, yeah, we're a boring old married couple."

"You could never be boring. How about a night of Texas Hold 'Em?"

"We'd love to. Does Tammy play?"

"Mostly online, but she does know the game."

"Great, how about after dinner since I already have something in the crock pot?"

"Perfect. Does seven work?"

"We'll be there."

After I disconnect the call, I turn saying, "There you go. They're both good. They'll let you know if they have any tips or notice any tells."

"I can't wait. And speaking of dinner, what would you like?"

"I could really go for meatloaf double beatloaf."

That earns me the cutest little giggle. "Okay, but only if you wear a pink bunny suit for me."

"Wrong character."

"Oh, I know. Don't ever challenge my knowledge of A Christmas Story! I just wanna see you in the suit."

"Yeah, not gonna happen."

"Party pooper!" She laughs

"Hey, I love you, but even I have a line." I grin

"Fair enough."

"Do you have what you need for the meatloaf?"

"No, I'll have to stop at the store on my way home."

"Ready to head out?"

"Yeah, I wanna make sure I have time to get everything done before our guests arrive."

"Great, meet you at home."

Tammy heads off to the store while I head home. I'm sitting out back when I hear Tammy's car. I gather up the dogs and take them inside. She's just finishing unpacking the bags and setting up everything she needs. I see the ingredients for the meatloaf, plus bags of potatoes and fresh spinach.

"Looks like I'm in for a treat tonight."

"I thought I'd do mashed potatoes and spinach for the sides."

"Yum. Now, put me to work."

"Okay. I'll get the meatloaf together if you don't mind peeling the potatoes. Peelers are not made for lefties."

"Not you, too. How come I never noticed?"

"Got me! That whole time we played Pictionary, and you never saw what hand I was using?"

"I'm a dunce!"

She laughs and hands me the peeler. "Well, this is your penance."

In what seems like no time, she has the meatloaf ready. I see her put a paper plate on the counter and fill it with a layer of bread crumbs. She rolls the entire loaf in the crumbs. "How come you do that?"

"A trick my gramma taught me. It makes a delicious crust on the might."

"I've never seen anyone do that before."

"You'll never wanna eat it another way again."

I finish up the potatoes, and Tammy hands me a knife. "Get the pieces as close to even as possible so they cook right. They need to be soft to make them mash better."

"Yes, ma'am."

The oven beeps, indicating it's done preheating, so she puts the pan inside. After I finish cutting the potatoes, she puts them in a pot with water, and cooks them until they're soft. No electric mixer for my girl. She takes a hand-masher out of the drawer and gets to work.

"I didn't know I had one of those."

"You didn't. Gramma left all her kitchen stuff, including her top secret recipe box, to me in her will. My mom was never interested in cooking. Gramma was so happy I wanted to learn since she never got to teach my mom."

"Aww, I love stories like that."

"She would have loved you. But you would have had to be careful. She liked to pinch the bottoms of handsome men. And you are quite pinch-worthy!"

"Well, I would not have complained. She sounds so sweet."

"She really was. I could never talk to my mom about anything. She was all business. The sad thing is, Gramma said she wasn't like that until she met my dad. So, Gramma was more like a mom to me. Any time I needed an ear, she was there. When she got sick, I was devastated. I became her caretaker in my sophomore year in high school."

"That's so young to have that kind of responsibility."

"I know that now, but at the time, I didn't hesitate. There was nobody else. I was the only one there when she passed away. I've always been so grateful that it was peacefully in her sleep. But, it was a hard thing to handle with no family support."

"How did you manage everything?"

"She was an active member of a local women's knitting group. The other ladies in that group were my angels. They helped me with everything. I had control of all the money, so I could pay all the expenses, but they helped me make all the arrangements. A few of the women who were younger at the time are still alive. They all live together as room-mates, like on *The Golden Girls*. I still try to visit when I can."

"I'd like to join you sometime."

"Okay, but remember what I said about your butt. They're pinch-ers, just like Gramma."

"I can handle it."

"Okay, but I'm not responsible for any butt bruises," she teases. Tammy gets out one of my skillets and puts a little olive oil in it. She puts in the fresh spinach and cooks that. While she gets all the food ready to serve, I set the table.

"Wow, this is delicious. I'm definitely glad your grandmother taught you to cook."

"Definitely some of my fondest memories. She was my best friend growing up."

After we're done eating, I give my girl a hug and help her put all the leftovers in containers. We feed the dogs and take them out back to run while we wait for Judd and Mel. A little before seven, I hear a round of barking and laugh as two furry flashes enter the backyard. All five dogs are running laps. Tammy's Sadie might be the smallest, but she's also the fastest, and she quickly out-laps the others.

When they're done playing, we take them inside. After they empty all the water bowls, they lay down together in the corner of the living room and we're treated to a loud round of snoring. Five sets of paws are twitching as they dream of chasing bunnies and squirrels.

We head down to the den, leaving the door open in case the dogs want to wander down. I get out a large silver case and open it. Tammy's face lights up when she sees poker chips in every color. There's also a deck of cards and a dealer button. I'm starting to get excited. I've been careful to downplay her skills. Mel and Judd will never know what hit them!

After I count out four equal stacks of chips, I take the cards out of the box, and I'm about to shuffle when Tammy stops me.

"That's NOT how you start a poker game," she says in her most serious voice.

"Oh, is that so? Well, then, educate me."

"Shuffle up and deal!" Tammy calls out.

Judd's eyebrows shoot up, and he glances over at Mel. I can't help but notice Mel's mouth hanging open. I hear an evil laugh in my head. Just you wait, my friend!

Going around the table, Judd is to Tammy's left, then Mel, and, finally, me. I deal each of us our hole cards. Tammy takes a quick peek at hers, but her face doesn't change. Judd's the big blind, so he checks. Mel, as the small blind, limps in with a call. Either they're trying to show weak hands, or they really have nothing. Tammy calls and I fold.

I deal the first three community cards, also called the flop, a nine, an ace, and a two. Still no change in Tammy's face, so I have no idea if the flop is any good for her. Mel and I both check, and Tammy puts a small bet in. Judd sits up a little straighter. Judd calls, and Mel folds.

I deal one card, the turn. Another two comes. This time, Judd bets but it's only a quarter of the pot TammyI raises to half the pot, and his eyes go wide. After a couple minutes of staring at Tammy, he finally calls.

I deal the last card, the river, and it's a four. The board has all four suits, so there's no way Judd can have a flush. Now I'm especially curious if Tammy has a good hand/ When she makes a big, bold move on the first hand, and shoves her remaining stack of chips in, I'm pretty sure she does.

"I'm all in," Tammy announces.

Judd wisely cuts his losses, and he folds. Tanny turns over two nines, giving her a full house and Judd nods in approval. "Well, looks like we have a shark on our hands," Judd says. "Holdin' out on us, Jay?"

"No way, man. She told me she watched and played some online, but that was it. The little hustler got me, too." I pretend to be annoyed, but I can't wipe the smile off my face.

"Oh, nice poker face," Tammy teases.

We all laugh. It doesn't take long for Mel and I to bust out. Tammy's won so many hands, Judd doesn't have enough chips to cover the big blind, so he has no choice but to go all in. And it could not have happened at a worse time. He turns over a pair of jacks. The smirk on his face quickly disappears when Tammy has two queens.

Right now, she's dominating, but the flop changes things when a jack comes up, along with a two and a six. That gives Judd a three of a kind. The turn gives us a four. Unless Tammy gets lucky, and a queen comes, the game will continue. I deal the river, face down at first.

"Before I flip this card over, I need to say that this has been so much fun. Whatever happens, this has been an awesome game."

I flip the card over, and Tammy squeals. All four of us sit there dumbfounded as we stare at the queen of hearts. Judd stands up and holds his hand out, which Tammy accepts. "Amazing game," Judd says.

"Thanks, but be honest, that last hand was all luck," Tammy says.

"True, but it was your skilled play in the previous hands that left me in that position. I'm impressed. You're gonna kick ass in AC if you play like that."

"Thank you."

"I don't know whether to be happy or sad that you beat my hubby," Mel says with a wink.

"Oh, I'm sorry. Now, I feel bad. But it was just for fun," Tammy says.

"What do you mean? We all owe you money."

"Oh, no. I couldn't. I thought this was just a fun game," Tammy says.

"Well, if you're sure," I say.

"I am. I just wanted a chance to practice before our trip. I definitely don't want to take advantage of you and your friends."

"Our friends, my love," I correct. Tammy smiles. "I guess we should head up and check on the dogs."

"Go ahead. I'll clean this up," Tammy says.

I follow Judd and Mel up the stairs to the living room. Not one dog has budged.

"She's so sweet, but I feel like there's still part of her that believes all the stuff Martin has said," Mel says quietly.

"I think so, too. I'm working on it. She's so special, and I'm not gonna give up until she truly believes it. And you can definitely help with that."

"That's part of what my standing girl-date nights with her are for. Plus, we really have fun together," Mel says.

"I'm so glad," Jay says.

"Well, guess we oughta head home," Judd says.

"I'll grab the leashes," I say.

"Leashes?" Tammy asks. Her head tilts to one side like the dogs, and it's so cute.

"Surprise! You didn't think it would only be a short, weekend trip, did you?" I say.

"Well, yeah. That's what you said."

"I'm a man of many surprises. Just you wait!"

Mel has a gleam in her eye, but she doesn't spoil any of what I told her. She and Judd get their two dogs while Tammy and I take our three out to their truck.

"Thank you both so much for this," I say.

"Have fun," Mel says with a wink.

After we head back inside, Jay says, "You have some packing to do my love."

Chapter Twelve

Tammy

The next morning, Jay carries our luggage downstairs. We're sitting in the living room. He won't let me eat breakfast, but he won't tell me why. My mind starts wandering to the ocean that I can't wait to see when a car horn interrupts my thoughts.

"Your chariot awaits, m'lady."

"Why, thank you, good sir."

Jay grabs our bags, so I open the front door. My jaw drops when I see a white Cadillac Escalade Limo in the driveway. The driver walks over and takes the bags from Jay. He loads them in the back. He pushes a button, and what looks like the door on a jet opens for Jay and I to get in the car.

I look around and I can barely believe my eyes. The limo is big enough to hold at least twenty people and wraps all around the inside. There's ways to connect pretty much any device you could think of. Jay plugs in his cell, opens the Spotify app, and puts some music on. Holy hell, it sounds like we're front row at a concert.

And that's not even all. I've never seen anything like this. There's a wood dance floor in the middle. The ceiling is full of LED lights, and there's one crazy light show going on, not to mention the two bars at each end. Not one bar. Two bars. This is insane.

"Oh my god, Jay. I don't even know what to say."

"It's amazing! Nothing but the best for my girl. Now, I'm sure you're wondering why I wouldn't let you have breakfast."

"Yeah, kinda. And of course, my mind went right back to Martin when he wouldn't let me eat."

"Wait! What did you just say?"

"Yeah, he said the fat pig could skip a meal from time to time."

"It's getting harder and harder not to deck him."

"For me, too, thanks to you."

"That's my girl. But you know that's not my reason."

Jay gets up and walks over to one of the bars. He produces a small fruit and cheese plate.

"Wow, that looks delicious."

"As do you."

I smile as I feel my cheeks heat up. Maybe someday, I'll stop blushing. But then again, maybe not. Either way, I'm getting more used to hearing nice things about myself. And it never escapes my attention that he's easily the hottest man I've ever seen.

"What can I get you to drink?" Jay asks.

"I don't suppose there's any coffee?"

'I had them put iced coffee and your favorite hazelnut creamer in the fridge."

"You really do think of everything."

Jay fixes two cups of coffee. He hands me one, and I take a sip. "This is perfect!"

I grab a small plate and put a couple pieces of cheese along with a pile of strawberries and blueberries. I know it sounds crazy, but I'd swear everything tastes more delicious than usual.

"Mmm. So yummy."

I lay my head on Jay's shoulder as we enjoy the two hour ride to Atlantic City. Our driver pulls into the VIP drop off in the valet area. The jet door opens, and I see a bellhop named Steven with a fancy gold luggage cart waiting for us.

"Mr. Donnelly, your suite is ready," Steven says.

"Thank you, sir," Jay says.

One of the things I admire most about Jay is how respectful he is toward other people. There's little I like less than people who look down on those in service roles. I definitely experienced plenty of that as a waitress. We follow Steven to the VIP check-in. I've never even come close to this kind of treatment, and I'm so afraid I'm gonna say or do something stupid like Vivian, Julia Roberts' character from *Pretty Woman*.

After Jay finishes checking in, we follow Steven to the elevators. "Your suite is in the South Tower as you requested."

"Is there a difference?" I ask. I feel stupid the second I finish the question. "Sorry, that must have sounded dumb."

"Not at all. I looked at both and opted for this tower because that's where the casino and the restaurants are."

"Well, that makes sense. Thanks for not making me feel dumb."

"Ma'am, if I might interrupt, the only dumb question is the one you don't ask. Always remember that," Steven says.

"Thank you," I say as I smile at him.

We arrive at the elevator bank. Jay scans his key at the security kiosk, and we wait for one of the elevators to reach the ground floor. Steven holds the door open for us to enter, then pulls the luggage cart inside and selects the button for the top floor. We reach the top floor, and he walks us to our suite.

Jay opens the door and says, "After you, my love."

I walk inside, and I have yet another jaw-dropping moment. I'm surprised my face hasn't frozen like this yet. It would take me weeks to make a list of everything this room features. I start exploring, and my eyes go wide when I see the master bath. There's a glass-enclosed shower stall next to a soaking tub big enough for at least four.

"I take it the tub is to your liking."

"Oh yes. I always loved bubble baths, but it's been so long, I'd probably forget how."

"Well, my dear, I think we'll have to figure that out together. I'd love to enjoy a bath with you, if you'll allow."

"I'd love nothing more."

"Wait, not even a bit of hesitation?"

"No, and that's thanks to you."

"You need to stop giving me all the credit. Yes, I know I helped. But, I did not fix you. I helped you find the courage to let that butterfly out of her cocoon. Baby, you had to want to do this. If you didn't, nothing I did, nothing I said would have made a damn bit of difference. But like I told you before, you are a badass superhero! I think we need to give you a name."

"Hmm. Oh, wait. I know. The Badass Butterfly! My costume can come complete with wings."

"I love it. We'll have to keep that in mind for Halloween."

My brain stops for a minute. It's only summer, and he's thinking about months from now. He still sees us together, something I'm not used to. How can he be so completely opposite of Martin? The old me would say I don't deserve someone like Jay. Well, you know what? Yeah, I fuckin' do. I fought like hell to get here, and it's about time for some good to come my way.

Without another word, I walk over to where he stands. With two fists, I grab his shirt and pull him to me. I plant a kiss so passionate on his sexy lips that I hear him growl into my mouth like a hungry tiger. And I intend to feed that tiger in my own special way later. But not right now.

"How about a nice long soak before we head down for dinner and some gambling?" I say.

Jay just stares at me, unable to even blink. "Holy shit. That kiss, woman."

"That's just a small preview of what's in store for you later."

"I've created a monster."

"Yeah, you have, and she's insatiable."

"Just the way I like it, baby."

I start to walk into the bathroom to get the tub ready. "Oh, no, you don't. This trip is about me pampering you. Please, make yourself comfortable while I get things ready."

I sit down on the couch and gaze out at the ocean. It looks so small from up here. All I can think about is walking along the beach, holding hands with Jay. I've always wanted to swim in the ocean, but like so many other things, I never had the courage to buy a bathing suit. But no more. And since a one-piece hides my scar, it helps me feel less self-conscious. I'm so lost in my own thoughts, I jump out of my skin when I hear a deep voice say, "The bubbles are ready."

I walk into the bathroom and my eyes immediately go to the naked god standing in front of me. Damn, he's perfection. I undress and walk over to the tub. Jay holds my hand as I walk up the steps. Such a gentleman. Well, except when we're in bed, but that's the way I like it! I ease myself down into the warm bubbly water and it feels like heaven.

I lay my head back on the rolled up towel Jay placed there and close my eyes. I feel his presence when he climbs in next to me. I can feel his body touching mine and it sends like electric shocks through my body. His touch excites me like nothing I've ever felt.

It's not long before I hear Jay snoring. Apparently, it's catching and I feel my eyelids getting heavy. I'm awakened by Jay's hand light lightly stroking my arm. "Baby, let's do a quick rinse off in the shower then get ready to head downstairs."

"Sounds great. Where are we eating? I wanna make sure I dress appropriately."

"Everything is taken care of."

After our rinse, I walk into the bedroom and see a garment bag hanging, with a smaller bag in front of it. When on earth did he have time to do this? And how did I not hear anyone come in. I put on one of the lingerie sets Mel helped me pick out on our shopping date. I take the garment bag down and open the summer.

An emerald green shimmery full length evening down looks back at me. I look inside the smaller bag and see a pair of low heel dress shoes and two felt boxes. Jay walks out, a huge smile on his face. "When did you do this? How did you know what size?"

"Well, as far as the size, I had some help. As far as when, I had everything sent here after I purchased it, with specific instructions on when it should be brought to the room. There's a bag for me, too."

Jay opens a second garment bag, and I see a black tuxedo inside. The bowtie and cummerbund are the same shade of green as my dress. He wasn't kidding about pampering me. I have a fleeting moment of feeling like I don't deserve this, but I push that aside. I'm working really hard to stop putting myself down. So, yes, dammit, I do deserve this!

I see in the bag there's a pair of thigh-high, sheer, black silk stockings. I pull them on, and then put the dress on. It fits perfectly. I can't believe this is my first thought, but I feel beautiful. Even a month ago, I wouldn't have been able to think that. I slip into the shoes and walk to the full-length mirror in the bedroom. I'm awestruck at the reflection looking back at me.

I hear a knock on our door. "Right on time," I hear Jay say. "I have another surprise for you, my queen. Are you dressed?"

"Yes, please come in."

Jay opens the door, and I hear a low, growly wolf whistle. Standing behind him are two women in long black smocks. "Meet Zoe and Maddie, hair and makeup."

"Hello," I say.

The ladies both smile. "This will be an easy one. You're already so stunning, we don't have much to do," Maddie says.

"Thank you. I'm only recently starting to believe that."

"Really? Why?" Zoe asks.

"Let's just say my ex-husband was not a nice man."

They both nod.

"I understand there's a special accent for your hair. I'd like to put it on you so I can decide how to style you," Zoe says.

I guess that must be one of the boxes in that bag I haven't opened yet. I get the larger box, and I see a gold tiara with diamond and emerald stones. I hand it to Zoe.

"Wow, beautiful," she says. She holds it up to my head and studies my hair for a few minutes. "I know exactly what to do. Please have a seat."

I sit down on the small bench in the bathroom. Zoe puts a cape on me to protect my dress. After a few quick snips, Zoe pulls all of my hair up and piles it on top of my head. She puts the tiara in place and steps back. "What do you think, Maddie?" Zoe says.

"I love it! What about you, Tammy?"

I turn and look in the mirror. Wow! "It looks great. I love it."

"Wonderful," Zoe says, a big smile on her face. "You're up, Maddie."

Maddie walks over to me, a large plastic box in her hand. She opens it, and I see every type and color of makeup in existence. There's also a ton of brushes, most of which I have no idea what to do with. "Well, I'm clearly an idiot when it comes to makeup," I say with a sigh.

"Don't say that," Maddie says. "A natural beauty like you doesn't need it anyway. All I'll be doing is applying a little color to enhance the color of your eyes. I have a social media channel with how-to videos if you ever want some tips."

"Thank you," I say, looking at the card with the QR code Maddie hands me.

She takes only a few minutes to work her magic, and I can't believe what I see when I look in the mirror.

"So, what do ya think?" Maddie asks.

"I love it. You can't even tell I'm wearing anything."

"That's exactly how it should look."

"Stand up and let's see the full you," Maddie says. I stand straight and tall, proud of how I look, proud of my height, proud of so much.

They both clap and bounce. "You really are stunning," Zoe says.

"Yeah, and I'm especially jealous about your height. I'd give anything to be a little taller. I'm only five foot three," Maddie says.

"I'm five foot nine. I love it now, but when I was younger and taller than all the other kids, well, I didn't have many friends."

"Well, considering the way we saw that hunk out there looking at you, I think you're good now!" Zoe says.

We all laugh before Maddie walks over and opens the door. She and Zoe walk out.

"Excuse us, Mister Donnelly," Zoe says. "We'd like to present your beautiful queen."

I walk out and Jay's jaw drops. "Holy hell, woman. And you ladies, wow. You did an amazing job."

"She made it easy. When you're working with such a beautiful canvas, it's easy to create a masterpiece," Maddie says.

"Thank you both so much." Jay reaches into the inside pocket of his jacket and pulls out two envelopes, handing one each to the ladies.

They smile and thank him in unison. Once they gather their stuff, they head out.

"Dinner awaits, my love. But before we go, I have another surprise for you."

Jay walks into the bedroom and returns with the smaller felt box. He opens it, and I see emerald earrings and a diamond tennis bracelet,

"Oh, Jay, they're beautiful."

"I can't wait to see them on you."

"Oh, I can't accept these. You've already done too much."

"No such thing."

He hands me the earrings, and I put them in. He takes my arm and fastens the bracelet. "Wow."

"Thank you," I say with a small curtsy.

Jay stands next to me and takes out his phone. He snaps a selfie of us and sends it to Mel and Judd. He shows me the picture, and even I have to admit we make a stunning couple. I just hope this isn't all a dream. If it is, I don't wanna wake up.

Chapter Thirteen

Jay

Her arm linked through mine, Tammy and I walk to the Council Oak Steaks & Seafood Restaurant. Tammy looks nervous when she sees how upscale the restaurant is. "You okay, honey?"

"Just afraid I'll send escargot flying through the restaurant." I laugh, and I see her body relax a bit. She'll be fine. Heads turn as we walk up along the path to the restaurant. All eyes are on my butterfly. Her red hair with the gold tiara and the emerald dress are such a stunning combination, I also can't stop gawking at her.

We walk to the maitre-d stand. "May I help you, sir?"

"Yes. I have a reservation under the name Jason Donnelly."

"Ah, yes, Mister Donnelly. Your table is ready. Please follow me."

"Thank you."

We walk to the table, and the maitre-d pulls Tammy's chair out slightly. She smiles at him and sits down. He looks surprised as he smiles back. I can't help but assume he deals with a lot of snooty women, but that's not my girl.

"Thank you," Tammy says.

SAMANTHA MICHAELS

"My pleasure. And may I say how refreshing it is to be treated like a human being."

"Well, you are a human being, so I wouldn't treat you any other way."

He bows slightly and approaches one of the waiters. I can see him saying something, but I can't make out what. When our waiter, Thomas, approaches, he smiles and says. "I've been informed that I must take extra-special care of you. Thank you for being so kind. Now, what can I bring you both to drink?"

I look at Tammy, hoping she'll give me some hint of what she wants to drink.

"May I have a glass of Moscato, please?"

"Good choice. What brand?"

A look of panic crosses her face. "A bottle from your top shelf," I say.

"Very well."

Thomas returns with a bottle of wine and two glasses. He pours us each a glass then places the bottle in the ice bucket next to the table. This is the first time I've seen Tammy have a drink, and I'm glad. I didn't want to push her if she wasn't comfortable, so I'm glad she was willing to order first.

"I'll give you a few moments with the menu," Thomas says.

"I'm afraid I'll say something dumb. Will you order for me?" Tammy asks.

"Of course, but you know you won't sound dumb. What would you like?"

"Well, it depends on what you're willing to let me spend."

"Oh, darling, there is no limit. Order what you want."

"Well, then, I would love filet mignon. Medium."

"And for a side?"

"Creamed spinach."

Thomas returns, and I order both meals. While we wait, all I can do is sit and stare.

"You're making me nervous. Is something wrong with my face?" Tammy asks.

"Why would you ask that?"

"Because you keep staring at me."

"That's because you're so beautiful."

"Well, you're as handsome a man as I've ever laid eyes on."

"Why, thank you, my love."

I see Tammy looking around the restaurant when suddenly, her eyes narrow to slits. I follow her gaze. What the fuck? It can't be. And great, he sees us, and now, he's heading this way. So help me, he upsets my girl tonight, and I won't be responsible for my actions. He gets to our table with a nasty smirk on his face.

"Well, well, well, behold the piggy princess," Martin says.

"Not tonight," I warn. "Just leave us alone."

"And if I don't?"

"Then you'll get a chance to taste my fist."

"Why do you still call me a pig when I've lost so much weight?" Tammy asks.

"Because you're ugly, worthless, and stupid."

She stands and faces him. With a slightly raised voice and her hands on her hips, she says, "I am not. You just never took the time to get to know me, to know what I'm capable of. Well, guess what? Jay has, and I've never felt better about myself."

"Oh, please give me a break. You will always deserve to feel like shit because you are, in fact, shit."

"No, Martin, I'm not. I let you treat me like that for far too long. I know what your real issue is. But I'll let you figure that out on your own. I just want you out of my life once and for all."

Hearing the commotion, the maitre'd approaches our table. "Pardon me, miss. Is this man bothering you?"

"Yes sir, he is. Would you be so kind as to have him removed?"

"It would be my pleasure ma'am." He radios for security and two very muscular guards approach our table moments later. They attempt to physically escort Martin out, but he pulls away, causing a fuss. Spinning around, he collides with a waiter carrying a large tray of food for a table of six.

Martin hits the floor, but not before he knocks the entire tray out of the waiter's hand. All of the plates come crashing down on Martin, leaving him covered with quite the variety of food. The guards get him up and drag him out as everyone watches. Tammy's trying her best not to laugh.

The maitre'd returns. "I apologize that you had to deal with that."

"It's not your fault," Tammy says. "My ex-husband refuses to leave me alone. I don't know if he knew we were coming here, or if it was a coincidence."

"Well, I have to say that not one of those things he said about you is true, miss."

"That's kind of you to say."

"I'd like to pay for the tray of food he destroyed," I say.

"We appreciate the offer, sir, but that won't be necessary. His bar tab was still open, so we informed him we would be adding the tray of food to his credit card before we closed it out."

"Very well," I say. I walk over to the table who was supposed to get the food and apologize on Martin's behalf.

One of the gentlemen at the table says, "We appreciate the gesture, but you are certainly not the one who should be apologizing. That disgusting man should be apologizing to your dinner partner."

"Thank you for saying that. Enjoy the rest of your evening."

I return to the table just as Thomas is bringing our food. Tammy just sits, not touching her food. "Everything okay?"

"Yeah, just feeling bad about earlier."

"I understand. I can sit here and say that you shouldn't, but I know you. Please just know that Martin is the one who was wrong. When I went to apologize to the diners whose meal was destroyed, the man I spoke with said the only one who should be apologizing is Martin to you."

"You know, you're right. I refuse to let him ruin this trip. Besides, the food smells divine, and I'm starving."

"That's more like it."

We finish our meals and another glass of wine each. Thomas approaches with the dessert menu. "Can I interest either of you in dessert or coffee?"

"Would you be okay sharing?" Tammy asks.

"I'd love to. What would you like?"

"The twenty-four karat chocolate cake," Tammy says.

"And two coffees," I add.

"Great choice. I'll be back in a moment with your coffee."

"So, what made you decide on that?" I ask.

"I read how it was made, and wow. It's a cocoa sponge cake with French milk buttercream and a ganache glaze."

"Sounds decadent."

"It does. Definitely not something I would eat often, but for a special occasion like this, definitely."

"Special occasion?"

"For so many reasons, especially being my first time here, and my first time on a trip with you."

"I love you."

"I love you, too."

After we finish dessert, I pay the check. "We need to get going. I have another surprise for you."

"Oooh. I'm so excited."

"I know you're gonna love this one."

I take Tammy to the players club booths so we can each get a card to track our gameplay. After we're done there, we head back to the casino floor. I stop at a section that has a small flight of stairs.

"That says high roller area," Tammy exclaims.

"I know. That's where we're playing tonight."

"But, Jay, I can't do that. That's too much for me."

"Do you trust me?"

"Yes, of course."

"Then come with me."

We walk up to the entrance of the high roller area. The attendant at the velvet ropes asks for my name. I give her my name, as well as Tammy's.

"Ah, yes, Mister Donnelly, you're all set. Please report to the sign-in table."

I take Tammy's hand and walk her to the table. Another attendant is checking players in.

"Okay, what's going on?" Tammy asks.

I look at her and wink, but I don't say anything.

"Player's name?" the attendant asks.

"Tammy Foster," I say.

"Welcome. I see your fifty thousand dollar entrance fee has already been paid. All players have been assigned random seats, so just look for the chip tray with your name."

"Thank you," I say.

Tammy hasn't said a word.

"Why so quiet?" I ask.

"I'm confused."

"About?"

"What's going on here?"

"Easy! You're playing in a poker tournament."

"W-w-what? I can't do that."

"The hell you can't."

"But -"

"Nope. No but."

Tammy walks around the table, checking out the other eight names. She stops dead in her tracks when she sees who's three seats to her left.

"It can't be."

"Oh yes it can."

"You knew?"

"Yep."

Tammy mentioned once in passing that Antonio Esfandiari was her favorite pro. When I saw he was playing in this tournament, I had to get her entered.

"Well, even if I lose to him, I'm excited to meet him."

"From what I was told, there will be a reception after the game for the players and whoever's here with them, so you'll get a chance to talk to him then."

"So, this is why the dress and all the primping?"

"Only partially. But most important to me was you being the center of attention, You deserve it. And you got the bonus of seeing a certain moron make an ass of himself."

"That was a definite highlight."

The rest of the players start making their way inside, and pretty soon, all nine seats are accounted for. One of the attendants grabs a microphone. "All players take your seats. Friends and family, please fill in the chairs to the right and left of the table. I give Tammy a kiss for good luck and find an empty seat.

The only woman at the table, she takes a seat. It only takes about thirty seconds for the first neanderthal comment. Looking Tammy up and down, the pig two seats over say, "We'll be down to eight pretty quickly. You could just divide up your chips now, honey, and save yourself the embarrassment."

Tammy lays her head on her hands and bats her eyelashes at the jerk. He's in deep shit now! The first hand comes down to him and Tammy. She's been betting modestly, and remembering back to our game with Judd and Mel, I think she has a good hand. Neanderthal man apparently picks up a different bag, as he pushes his entire stack in, a smug look on his face.

Tammy calls, and the jerk laughs, thinking he just tricked her. He flips over an ace and a king. The board has an ace, king, six, nine, and two. Tammy's expression remains serious as she slowly flips over one ace. If she has a king, they split the pot. But if she has the last ace, she's got him. She flips the other card, and I jump out of my seat when I see the second ace.

Tammy stands and attempts to shake the eliminated player's hand. He spits on the floor next to her feet and storms off. A security guard walks over. "That behavior is unacceptable. You'll need to leave."

One by one, the other players eventually bust out until Tammy and poker pro, Antonio Esfandiari, are head to head. After several exciting hands, trading chips back and forth, Antonio has a one thousand dollar chip lead over Tammy. The dealer deals the next set of hole cards to both players.

Tammy's the small blind and first to act. She does a quick peek at her cards and raises. Antonio re-raises and Tammy calls. The flop shows a king, jack, and a two. For the remaining rounds of betting, Antonio is first to act. He bets, and after another peek at her cards, Tammy raises. Antonio snap calls. The turn gives us a queen and I start having flashbacks to the final hand between Tammy and Judd.

Antonio places a pot size bet, and I can hear a quiet gasp ripple through the crowd of spectators. I'm starting to fear that Antonio has a king, but he could also be bluffing a weak hand. This time, Tammy snap calls. The final card comes up. A second queen. Is it possible? Could she have done it again? It won't quite end the tournament, but Antonio will have to go all in just to cover the small blind.

Antonio goes all in. No way he's bluffing. He wouldn't risk leaving himself a short stack if he had nothing. It all comes down to Tammy's cards. She looks at her cards one last time and Antonio gives a slight smile. He must see that as weakness. She calls, and his eyebrows shoot up. For the first time in this hand, he looks a little nervous.

Antonio shows two kings, giving himself a full house, kings over queens. Some light applause comes from his cheering section as everyone assumes he's won. I watch Antonio's face as Tammy turns over her cards. Two queens. I hear a boo come from somewhere behind me. I stand up, turn, and glare. The booing stops. Antonio gives her a nod before he pushes his remaining one thousand chips in front of him. Tammy puts out the same amount and the cards are dealt face up to each player since no additional betting can occur.

Tammy wins the hand with top pair. She and Antonio both stand and walk to either side of the attendant. "Thank you to all of our players for an exciting game. It was an honor to have a pro with us. And now, I'd like to officially congratulate our winner, Tammy Foster."

"Thank you so much. I had a great time."

Antonio motions for the microphone. "Miss Foster, congratulations on a wonderfully played game. I'm never a fan of losing, but it was an honor losing to someone with such talent."

"Thank you. I've been a fan of yours for quite a while, to say this was my honor is an understatement. I told my boyfriend I would have been okay losing just to get the chance to play with you, though I must say, I'm glad I didn't."

Antonio laughs and shakes her hand. He gives the microphone back to the attendance, who makes a small announcement.

"For those on the guest list, along with our players, well the eight of our players who are still here tonight, we're having a small reception in this room. Sit tight, and give us a few moments to set things up. For everyone else, thank you for watching tonight's tournament."

The host asks if we want our winnings now or to have them held in the casino safe. I let them know to hold them and we'll pick them up before we leave.

During the reception, Tammy gets a few minutes to chat with Antonio, and I'm impressed at how she handles herself. He signs her entry form for her. After the reception, we head out of the high roller area. "Where to now, my queen?"

"Well, um, do you like to dance?"

"I love to. And I was hoping you would, too. I booked us a VIP reservation at The Balcony."

We head to the club, and I check in at the VIP desk. We're escorted to a private area. We get a personal server and a VIP host.

"This is amazing. Every time I think I'm experiencing the most amazing thing of my life, you hit me with something else. Are you sure I'm really worth all this?" Tammy asks.

"I brought you here, right?"

"Yeah."

"Then there's your answer. And I wanted to do this tonight, as the music theme is eighties dance hits."

As we're sitting, *Heart of Glass* by Blondie comes on. I see Tammy's eyes fill with tears.

"This song bringing back some memories?"

"Yeah, good ones."

"Tell me."

"I know I've told you how much fun I had cooking with my grandma. Well, I had some fun with my grandpa, too. He taught me all about cars. He was the original owner of the very first Mustang that was sold, the nineteen sixty-four and a half. The car was factory original, including an eight track player."

"Oh, how cool!"

"Yeah. I know how to work on them and how to drive a stick shift. Grandpa and I would go out for Sunday drives. He was into all the eighties music. So, we'd cruise around blasting eight tracks of Blondie, his favorite band."

"I'm really sorry I'll never get to meet them. They sound like the coolest grandparents ever."

"They definitely are. Grandpa's plan was to leave the car to me, but when he passed, I wasn't yet eighteen, so he left it to my mom. He had added a request that the car be held for me until I was an adult, but my mother wasn't required to comply. And she didn't."

"She kept it?"

"No. I coulda lived with that because it would have stayed in the family. Instead, after researching what that car in pristine condition could fetch, she sold it. I was gutted. I would give anything to own that car. Not one like it, but the actual car that was my grandpa's. But, I can't dwell on that now. Let's hit the dance floor."

I have a new mission when I get home.

We head down to the dance floor, and I take Tammy's hands in mine as we spin around the dance floor. After a few more songs, we take a break and enjoy some water. I see Tammy yawn.

"What do you say we call it a night? You need to get some rest for tomorrow's adventure."

Chapter Fourteen

Tammy

"Now this is what I came here for," I say. Standing here in the cool morning air, looking out at the Atlantic Ocean, I feel at peace. There's something so magical about the ocean, something that's always called to me. I feel Jay take my hand as we get closer to the water.

"Wanna dip our toes in?"

"I do."

I love the feeling of the warm ocean water and wet sand between my toes as we walk to the edge of the water. I can see a couple of fishing boats off in the distance. I turn toward Jay and put my arms around him. He pulls me into one of his bear hugs, and the rest of the world disappears.

His lips brush mine. Not the hard crushing kisses he usually lays on me, though. This is soft, gentle, slow, and strangely enough, excites me even more than those hard passionate ones. Even his tongue is gentler. I truly believe the ocean has this calming effect on anyone who takes it in. And I'm glad Jay's one of those people.

Our kiss is interrupted by the sound of a boat getting closer. I open my eyes, and a pontoon boat is heading to the shoreline. The captain calls out, "Excuse me, I'm looking for Jason Donnelly."

"I'm Jason."

"I'm Captain Bernie Lomax. Are you ready to head out?"

"One moment. We just need to dry off and get our shoes back on."

"I'll be waiting."

After we board the boat and sit down on the soft leather sofa seats, the captain walks over to us.

"Everything you requested is in the cooler to your left. We'll spend the afternoon touring Barnegat Bay, and I'll drop you back here before dinner time."

"Thank you, Captain," Jay says.

"Yes, thank you," I add.

"My pleasure."

Captain Lomax starts the boat, and we're off.

"So, I see you brought your guitar today."

Jay takes his guitar out of the case and starts strumming. As always, his playing lulls me into a trance. As my ears enjoy the soft sounds of his guitar, my eyes take in the stunning sights as we tour. The sky is a bright blue, and there's not a cloud anywhere in sight. The sun shines brightly, and the temperature is just right in the low seventies.

"I could definitely handle living on the waterfront," I say.

"I've never told anyone this, but me too. I love the ocean. Yet another reason we were made for each other."

"There sure have been a lot of those. And I'm very happy about that."

"Me too."

Jay quietly starts singing *The Dock of the Bay* by Otis Redding.

"I love that song," I say. I start whispering the words, and Jay stops.

"Baby, how about a quick duet?"

"Oh, no, I'm a terrible singer."

"Like hell. I've heard you sing, and you're amazing. Now come on, sing with me."

Jay restarts the song, and this time, I join him. I have to admit, we do sound good together. I love singing, but it was yet another thing Martin told me I was awful at, so I stopped doing it. Why the hell I ever listened to him is beyond me.

When our tour is done, Captain Lomax takes us back to the beach in front of the Hard Rock. We thank him, and Jay hands him an envelope. We walk over to where we were standing this morning, and that's when I see a small round table and two chairs. A small vase with a single flower sits on the center of the table. There's a menu at each chair. We walk over and take a seat.

A waitress comes from the casino and takes our order. After we finish eating and Jay settles the bill, we go for a walk along the beach.

"I had so much fun singing with you today," Jay says.

"Me too. I always enjoyed singing, but I wasn't allowed to do it in the house."

"My god, this guy is horrible. I'm in awe that you survived him."

"That's all I did. Barely. But now, I'm living. Living my best life with the best man I've ever known."

"I always thought I was, too. I loved my job, my home, my life. But, I always had this nagging feeling that something was missing. Now I know it was someone not something. And I know that someone is you." Jay sits down in the sand. "Come join me baby."

He points to the empty sand between his legs. I sit down and lean back against his chest. He puts his arms around as we watch the sun start to set. The reflection on the water is breathtaking. Jay takes out his guitar and holds it in front of me.

"I can move so you have more room to play."

"Hey, none of that. I have plenty of room around that sexy little body of yours."

I hear the opening notes of *I'm Yours* by Jason Mraz, another of my favorite singers. I close my eyes as Jay sings, and a scene starts playing in my head. I see myself in Jay's kitchen, wedding band on my finger, cooking for him. Tammy Donnelly has a nice ring to it. I don't have any clue if marriage is something he's ever wanted to try. Hell, I have no idea if I would accept a proposal after how my first one went, but I don't hate the picture.

"Do you know any other songs by Jason? I'd love to sing one with you, and I have a certain one in mind," I say.

"I know them all. He's my guilty pleasure. Which one did you want to sing?"

"*Lucky*. I love the way he and Colbie Caillat's voices sound together."

"I love that one. But before we start, stand up with me."

This time, we pretend we're on a stage singing together. We're so wrapped up in singing together, we don't notice a small crowd had gathered until we were done. We're met with a round of applause that startled us both.

"Guess we sounded pretty good," I say.

"Like there was any doubt. And hey, this gives me an idea for our re-opening."

"Oh yeah, what?"

"A singing contest. Of course, we wouldn't be eligible, but we could kick it off with a duet."

"I love it! When we get home, I'll work out the details."

"Great. Now that ends the work talk."

"Agreed."

Jay puts his guitar back in the case. We walk a little bit more before heading into the casino. We decide to have a little fun at one of the penny slots. We win a small amount and cash out before heading back to our room.

"I believe I remember quite the kiss you laid on me last night."

"Oh, I remember it well. And now, I'm gonna show why I did it. I want you naked in that bed. Now."

"Oh, damn woman."

I watch as he unwraps his delicious body. I can't wait to taste him, touch him, have him inside me. Damn, this man. I leave a trail of clothes as I walk to the bed. I lay down. He tries to lay next to me, but I put my hand up.

"Nope. You're under my command tonight. Unless you have a problem with that."

"No, ma'am."

"Good. Then, get that head between my legs and make me squeal. Your tongue is like magic. Make me come like never before."

His tongue slides between my folds and holy shit. I cry out when he puts pressure on my clit. He circles it with the tip of his tongue. A little nip with his teeth drives me wild. He puts his lips around it and sucks so hard, it doesn't take long for me to explode. My body bucks up and down on the bed as I shake from head to toe.

"Please, I need you inside me now."

With one long, hard thrust, he fills me completely. He puts his hands down so I'm not bearing his full weight. I love being on top, but there's something so intimate about this position. He lowers his head so he can kiss me, and oh my god, there's that hard passionate kiss that sends me into orbit.

I feel him thrusting harder and faster, and I know I'm about to get a special treat. He unloads his hot lava inside me, and I sigh. He flops next to me, his sweat-soaked body glistening. So fuckin' sexy.

I loved the long, slow intimate encounter we shared our first time, but this one was just as exciting in its own way. To have someone want me so bad he can't control himself is nothing I ever thought I'd experience. And not once has he made me feel bad about my physical flaws. I'll always remember the kind words he said when he saw my scar.

"I wish we didn't have to leave tomorrow," I say.

"I know, and if we didn't have a lot to finish up at the bar, we wouldn't. But, the limo will be here early, so let's grab a quick shower and get some sleep. Breakfast will be provided in the limo tomorrow morning, so we can just check out and go."

"Promise me we'll come back again sometime."

"Not sometime, lots of times. That I can definitely promise."

After we pick up my winnings the next morning, a security guard escorts us to our limo, and we head home.

Chapter Fifteen

Jay

"I can't believe it's finally here," I say as I sit and enjoy the delicious omelet Tammy made me.

"I'm so excited for tonight, especially kicking off the singing contest with you. Are we still doing *Lucky*?"

"Absolutely, especially after the reaction we got that night on the beach."

"That was a pretty cool moment. I've had so many of them with you, thanks to you."

"Well, today, I'm the one who owes you a whole lot of thanks. I would never have been able to get everything ready without your help. You, my butterfly, are amazing."

"I love what I'm doing so much that it doesn't even feel like work."

"That's awesome. And even though it doesn't feel like work, it is, and you do an outstanding job. Once we have a couple weeks open, I have an assignment for you."

"Oh yeah, what?"

"I want you to evaluate the waitstaff and identify a potential lead and trainer."

"I can do that. I used to do all the training for Nick, so I know what it takes."

"Is everything set at the VIP table?"

"Yeah. It's still just Mel and Judd, and Allie and Dane, correct?"

"Yep. Mel was insistent that Allie be there. Mel always said she was the best assistant ever, and more importantly, she kept Mel informed of everything going on with Daniel."

"I remember one of your group outings. I could tell how much Dane and Allie adored each other."

"They really did. I'm glad she was able to keep her job at O'Laughlin when all the dust settled."

"That was one wild night. That's the type of thing you would only see on TV or in a movie. To actually be there witnessing was surreal. And that night was also the first night something started to stir inside me where you're concerned. One look at you in that tux, and wow."

"You never said anything."

"I was nowhere close to being confident then. I barely had the courage to even make eye contact with you, let alone tell you the effect you had on my panties."

"Who are you, and what did you do with the Tammy I first met?" I tease.

"She's never coming back. You're stuck with the new, and hopefully improved, version."

'You were always that version. You just needed to learn that, so I love all the prototypes that got us here."

"Geez, I thought I was a person, not a machine."

"Oh, you absolutely are a person. No machine has warm soft skin, lips that beg to be kissed, and an ass that feels so good in my hands."

"You're such a sweet talker."

We both laugh before we clean up the kitchen. We start getting a couple of bags packed for the dogs. I had one of the rooms upstairs built with soundproofing so the dogs had somewhere to be while we're at the bar.. With the room, their ears will be protected from the music and any other noise. We load up the dogs and all their stuff before heading out.

Tammy heads over to the kitchen area when we get inside. Prep is going well, so she gathers up the bartenders and wait staff. After a quick pep talk, which has them all smiling, she joins me.

"You're a natural leader. I'm so impressed. You would've done great at O'Laughlin."

"Thanks, babe. I'm gonna go grab the easel with the sign up board for the singing contest tonight. Be right back."

She heads back down a few minutes later and gets everything set up. "What else do we need to get ready?" she asks.

"Everything's all set at our VIP table, so let's get the welcome signs placed at all the other tables."

"Okay. I'll also have two sets of silverware placed at each table."

She walks over and again gathers up the waitstaff. They've all been given their sections, so they each get to work setting up their tables. I notice all of them hustling. Everything comes to a halt when there's commotion at the entrance.

"I told you, sir, you are NOT allowed in this bar. This is your last warning. If you don't leave voluntarily, I'll be more than happy to assist," Bruno, my head of security shouts.

It can only be one person. I walk over and get right in Martin's face. As loud as I can, I say, "Leave her the fuck alone."

"And if I don't?"

"Seriously, dude, are you listening to yourself? You sound like a damn baby. You had her, but you weren't man enough to keep her. Serving with divorce papers while she was in the hospital. How pathetic. Well, look at her now. She's thriving, and best of all, it's without you. I know you hate that."

"Yeah, so what? I could get any woman I wanted."

"Not any woman." I look and see Mel and Judd standing there.

"Wow, you're a cutie," Martin says as he looks Mel up and down. Judd's body stiffens as he moves closer to his wife.

"And you're a slug. Anyone who could treat someone the way you treated my friend deserves nothing but misery."

"You really need to learn to keep your woman in line," Martin says to Judd.

I don't know how he manages to keep it together and not deck Martin. Probably the same way I do, focusing on my girl. Bruno, on the other hand, has heard enough. Without a word, he picks Martin up and throws him over his shoulder. One of the other guards holds the door open, and we watch as Martin's ass hits the sidewalk.

"Leave the premises and don't return. Next time, we let the police handle it," Bruno says. He turns to Mel and says, "My apologies for his ignorant remark, Mrs. Walker."

"You're not the one who should apologize, but I appreciate it. And thank you for taking out the trash."

"My pleasure, especially when I heard how he treated Miss Foster."

Judd shakes Bruno's hand, and we let him get back to work.

I walk Mel and Judd to the VIP table where Tammy stands and waits for us. "Jay, are you sure you want me to stay working here?"

"Of course. Why wouldn't I? Oh, you don't think because of what just happened I'm having doubts, do you?"

"Well, yeah, kinda. What if he doesn't stop? What if he keeps trying over and over to get to me? Wouldn't it be better if it was somewhere else and not here messing with your business?"

"Absolutely not. This is our business, and I want you here. The days of that weasel controlling your life are over."

"Okay, but if you change your mind..."

"Hush!" I give her a kiss on top of her head.

"Can we please send him to be Daniel's roomie?" Mel jokes.

That gets a laugh out of everyone and helps Tammy relax. I hear the door open, and I see Mel take off running. She nearly knocks Allie over with a hug. I see her whisper something into Allie's ear. They both look at me and giggle.

"So, Jay, I hear you finally found someone willing to put up with you," Allie teases.

"I found the most amazing woman ever, no offense to you and Mel."

"None taken," Allie says. "Oh my god, Tammy. How are you? You working tonight?"

Allie has a Joey Tribbiani moment. Her eyes widen when she realizes. "Wait, you and him. Wow. I used to tell Dane how I thought you two looked good together, and now you are. I'm so happy for you both."

Allie gives Tammy a hug.

"Thanks," Tammy says. "It took a while for me to get here, all my fault, but this amazing man would not give up on me."

"They don't come much better than these three," Mel says.

"You got that right," Allie adds.

"Be careful, or those hats won't fit anymore," Tammy teases.

The girls all laugh while us three men try to put on an annoyed face. It doesn't work, and we're laughing right along with them.

"Please, everyone have a seat. We'll be back to visit when we can, but we still have a couple of things we need to check on before the doors open to the public," Jay says.

As we head over to the kitchen to make sure everything's set there, Tammy says, "Tonight's gonna be epic. I can feel it."

"Me too, baby."

The doors open at seven, and in no time at all, every table is full. Every bar stool is taken. I hate that we have to turn people away, but I don't need us getting shut down on the first night.

"Good idea," Tammy says. "I'm not singing a Blondie song to calm everyone."

"What are you talking about?"

"Oh, Jay. Don't tell me you've never seen Coyote Ugly."

"Can't say I have."

"Well, then you're gonna. Next movie night is my pick, so there you go! I picked."

"Sounds like a plan. And speaking of plans, what do you say we get this singing contest kicked off?"

"I'm ready!"

Tammy and I walk up on stage, and I grab a microphone. The DJ turns off the music so I can talk.

"Good evening, all. Thank you, everyone, for coming to our grand re-opening. We were nervous about the amount of guests we would get, but you've far exceeded our expectations. Now, it's time for you to provide some entertainment. For those of you who signed up for our singing contest, please report to the bar area. You'll be given instructions on what to do."

I hand the microphone to Tammy.

"But before that, everyone, we're going to kick things off with a duet. Of course, we aren't eligible for the contest, but we wanted to give our contestants a chance to warm up," Tammy says.

I grab my guitar and stand in front of a microphone stand, while Tammy holds hers. As I start the opening notes of *Lucky,* we start singing. We add a few small dance moves as we sing. Tammy's a natural on stage, and I can't help but wonder if there's anything she can't do. We finish the song to a loud round of applause, including a standing ovation from our friends. We exit the stage and join our friends while the DJ takes over and kicks off the contest.

"Wow, you two sound great together. I love that song," Mel says.

"It's one of my favorites," Tammy says.

"Me too. Jason Mraz is dreamy," Allie adds.

"Hey, I saw that he's playing at a casino in the Poconos toward the end of the summer. Maybe the three of us need a girls weekend."

"Oh my god, including tickets to his show?" Tammy exclaims.

"Of course," Mel says. "You in, Allie?"

"You bet I am," Allie says.

"Well, dudes, guess we'll have to figure out what we wanna do that weekend," Jay says.

"I think we should join the girls and make sure they behave," Judd teases.

Mel sticks her tongue out at her husband.

"I'm down for whatever you guys decide," Dane adds.

The rest of the night goes smoothly. After the staff cleans up, we let them all head home early with pay as a thank you for how hard they worked. Mel and Judd, and Allie and Dane head home leaving only Tammy, Bruno, and me left.

"Bruno, you're welcome to head home."

"Not until you two do, sir. I don't want Martin to try anything."

"I hope he won't be stupid enough to hang around," I say.

"It wouldn't surprise me," Tammy says. "Is there anything I can do?"

"Maybe a restraining order or protective order," Bruno says. "At least then he can be arrested for getting near you."

"I'll call my lawyer in the morning," I say.

"Thanks," Tammy sighs.

Tammy and I go upstairs to gather up the dogs, who are all curled up asleep. They look so cute together. All three of them bound down the steps, and by the time we get down there, they're all sitting in front of Bruno, as if they're his soldiers.

He takes one of the leashes while Tammy and I each grab one, and the three of us head outside. I turn on the alarm and lock up. Bruno walks us to my truck and waits until we're safely inside my truck and on our way out of the parking lot before he gets in his jeep.

"I'm not sure I'm built for night hours anymore," Tammy says when we get inside.

"I never was. But it was worth it for this."

"I'll get used to it again, I promise."

"If things go as planned, you won't need to for long. Part of why I want you to find a supervisor and trainer for the waitstaff is so they can be the night manager. That leaves you and I only needing to work day hours for the administrative stuff. And not full-time hours either."

"But, Jay, I need those hours. I can't afford to only work part-time."

"Come sit with me for a minute."

I walk over to the couch and Tammy joins me. "I was gonna surprise you with this in a few weeks, but I'm making you an equal partner."

"I can't afford that."

"That's not what this is about. I want to spend as much time with you as possible. I don't want us to be tied to the bar. So, please, do this with me."

"Okay." I hear the reluctance in her voice. But I'm happy she agreed. My goal is to spend the rest of my life spoiling this woman.

Chapter Sixteen

Tammy

"Thank you all for agreeing to come in an hour early each day this week. We've made it to Friday, and I have some exciting news. But first, a quick reminder that you will be paid additional wages, due to not having tipping customers. What we've been doing this week between these sessions and observing you all at work is looking for two people, one to be the trainer and one to be the supervisor," I say.

I look around and see mostly excitement on everyone's face. I do notice one of the waitresses, Nicole, looks a little nervous. Nicole started about two years ago and fit right in. I hope her nerves are because she really wants this, and not because she's afraid of being in charge.

"Before I make the official announcement, Jay and I are going to meet with each of you individually. Once all the meetings are done, we'll gather back down here for the official announcement. Please note that I'm calling you in alphabetical order by last name, so the first two people called are not necessarily the ones we've chosen."

****

I stand up front and address the team once more. "Everyone, please have a seat. After the announcement, we'll have a small reception before we get ready for the start of our shift. Everyone performed really well throughout, and we couldn't be more pleased with the staff we have here. We do, however, have two people that really stood out. First, please congratulate Vince on being named your new head trainer. He'll be responsible for training any new hires as well as coaching our current staff if the need arises."

Vince comes up front and stands with Jay and I, while the rest of the staff applauds. I glance over at Nicole, and the nervous look she had earlier is gone.

"And now, let's congratulate your new supervisor, Nicole."

As Nicole joins Vince and I up front, an even louder round of applause breaks out for Nicole, and her face lights up. After talking with her, I was especially positive I made the right choice. She said she wants to keep moving up, either here or somewhere else. I think she's a perfect candidate for Jay's tuition assistance program.

Jay joins us. "Congratulations to both of you. I completely agree with Tammy's choices. Our plan is to eventually leave the two of you in charge of the staff during the time the bar is open. Tammy and I will do most of our admin work during the day."

"But, not right away, correct?" Nicole asks.

"Correct. Tammy will be working with both of you on the skills and tasks to perform this role. We won't leave you on your own until you're ready. And you'll always be able to reach us if something happens."

"Who would be our go-to person here if we need something?" Vince asks.

"That will be Bruno. As head of security, he's linked into all the first responder services and the alarm copy for those types of situations. Anything he can't handle, he'll contact Tammy or me."

"Any other questions?" I ask.

Neither of them has anything now.

"I know this is cliche, but my door is always open any time you need to talk. There are days when it can get frustrating leading people. So, please don't ever hesitate to come to me if a situation comes up. I can coach you through how to handle it. Now, go join the rest of the staff and grab something to eat."

I watch as they join the rest of the team. Everyone is hugging and laughing. I love the dynamics of this group. It's a big part of why they do such an amazing job. One or two bad apples can ruin the bunch, but I haven't seen any signs that we have any.

****

"We need to talk about something," I say.

"What?"

"Things have been hectic, but don't think I've forgotten that my staying here is only temporary. I need to find somewhere permanent."

"Why can't it be here?"

"You've already been so generous to me. I can't keep taking advantage of you."

"I understand how you feel, but, baby, I don't wanna sleep without you. I love having your warm body next to me at night. And look how the three dogs have bonded."

"Well, I would just leave Sadie here. It would be hard, but I wouldn't pull her away from Lorelei and Sookie."

"Well, I don't want you away from me. Please, baby, live with me. I love you so much."

I really wanna say yes, but I'm hit with a sudden bout of fear. I sit down on the couch and stare at the wall. Jay sits next to me and gently rubs my arm.

"Talk to me, butterfly."

"I'm scared."

"Of me?"

"Oh, no, of course not. I hope you can understand where I'm coming from. Things were so bad for so long, that I had just resigned myself to the fact that was how my life was intended. Then Martin did me the biggest favor by divorcing me. I could finally live my life the way I wanted."

I stop for a minute, trying to read Jay's face, but he's giving nothing away.

"Then, I meet you and eventually fall head over heels in love with you. This is by far the happiest I've ever been, and it's beyond exciting. But it's also beyond scary. Like someone's taunting me, or I'm actually still under sedation, and this is all a dream. I'm so afraid I'm gonna wake up and still be married to Martin. Still in hell. Still hopeless."

"I see where you're coming from, but think about this. If you were living in a fantasy, wouldn't your grandparents still be alive?"

"Hmmm. Good point. If I was creating a dream life for myself, they would definitely be in it."

"Plus, I wouldn't. Mel and Judd wouldn't. You didn't know any of us before your medical emergency, so you would have no way to conjure us."

"Okay, so I know this is my real life. But, Jay, I still feel like someone's waiting in the wings to pull the carpet out from under me."

"I dare them to try. I'm not gonna pressure you, but baby, promise me you'll at least think about it."

"Truth is, I don't need to. I wanna be with you, too."

"So, you'll stay?"

"Yeah, I'll stay."

Jay jumps up from the couch and grabs me. He lifts me so my feet are no longer touching the floor and twirls me around. The dogs apparently think this is playtime, so they start running circles around us, barking and carrying on. Jay puts me down, and we take them out back so they have more room to run.

"Well, now that this is going to be your permanent home, we need to get the rest of those boxes unpacked. Now that things are going so well at the club, how about we take a couple of days off and get that done?" Jay says.

"Sounds like a plan. There's probably some stuff I can get rid of. I still have clothes from before. I'd rather get rid of those memories, so I was thinking we could donate them. There may be some other stuff, too, like if we have duplicates of things like kitchen stuff."

"That works."

****

After we finish, we pack up all the boxes of stuff to donate and take them to one of the local thrift shops. This one is my personal favorite. Any proceeds on the items they sell are donated to Habitat for Humanity.

When we get home, we take the rest of my clothes upstairs. Jay has two closets in his bedroom, so he clears one for me, and I get all of my clothes put away. We head back downstairs and get the rest of the boxes back. I plop down on the sofa, completely exhausted.

"You look like you could use a soak in the hot tub," Jay says.

"Oh, yes, please."

"Let's go!"

After a nice long soak in the tub, that of course included a nap, we head downstairs and grab some dinner.

"Guess what tonight is?" Jay says.

"What?

"Movie night. And look what I bought."

Jay hands me a bag. I look inside and see a DVD copy of *Coyote Ugly.*

"Yay! I can't wait for you to see it."

"Great. I'll make some popcorn, then we can head downstairs."

I take the dogs down and get them settled while I wait for Jay. We cuddle up together on the couch, and he starts the movie. He yawns at first, but I have a feeling when it gets to the part when Violet starts working at the bar, he'll change his mind. After all, how can you go wrong with hot women dancing on a bar?

By the end, he's into it, bopping along to the music, and I can't help but laugh. Once the credits start rolling, I look over at him, and he's grinning.

"So, what did ya think?"

"It was a little boring at first, but I ended up loving it. Maybe we should get you dancing on the bar."

"Yeah, not gonna happen. I'll sing on stage, but I will not do that."

"Fair enough. I hope you'll at least agree to dance for me sometime."

"Now, that I would consider. But I'd need to be properly motivated."

"Oh, I'd make it worth your while, butterfly."

"You up for another movie?"

"Maybe tomorrow. I'm exhausted tonight."

"Bed it is, my love. Our bed."

"I love the way that sounds."

Chapter Seventeen

Jay

Tammy's down at the club meeting with Vince and Nicole to get a progress report, so I'm hanging out in the living room with my laptop. I have quite the surprise brewing for my love. I hear the doorbell, and assume it's Mel and Judd. I open the door, and it's definitely not my friends.

Even though I've never met them, there's enough of a resemblance that I'm pretty sure I'm standing face to face with Tammy's parents. I decide to play dumb.

"May I help you?"

"We're looking for our daughter. Tammy," Tammy's mother says.

"And what makes you think she's here?"

"We know she is. We've been keeping tabs on her since we left. We know she's been working at the Saloon, and that you recently bought it," Tammy's dad says.

Anger starts to build.

"So, you've known where she is, and you're just now trying to contact her?"

"I'm not sure that's any of your business," her father says.

"You're right. It's not, but Tammy has the right to know."

"Then, can we see her?" her mom asks.

"That's up to her. She's not here, but let me call. Please wait outside."

After I shut the door, I dial Tammy's cell.

"Hey, Jay. I'm right in the middle of a chat with Nicole."

"Sorry to bother you at work, but we have a situation, and I'm not sure what to do."

I hear Tammy address Nicole. "Nicole, please excuse me for a few moments?"

"Of course. I hope everything's okay."

"Thank you."

I hear Tammy's office door close. "Okay, what's going on? Tammy asks.

"Um, I don't know how to tell you this."

"Just spill it."

"Your parents are outside."

"Excuse me? Did you say my parents?"

"Yeah."

"How did they know I lived there?"

"I asked, and your dad said they've always kept tabs on you."

"And they never once came to see while I was in the hospital?" she shouts. "Sorry, that's not your fault. I shouldn't yell at you."

"I know you weren't, sweets. But listen, they want to see you. I told them that was up to you and made them wait outside while I called you. Do you want to come home and talk to them, or should I send them away?"

"I have to admit I'm torn, but I am kinda curious why they decided to show up now. But if I do this, will you please stay with me?"

"What if they don't want me to stay?"

"Then they can leave. That's a dealbreaker."

"You got it, babe. I'll let them know."

"Thanks. I just need a few minutes to finish up with Nicole, then I'll be home."

"Okay. I'll be out back with them. I'm a bit leery of having them in the house until we see what they want.

"I agree."

****

My nerves kick in when I hear Tammy's car. I have no idea how she's going to react when she sees her parents. Whatever her reaction, my only focus is on her. If her parents are hurt by anything she says, that's on them for abandoning her.

She must be getting close based on three dogs going crazy. They race to the side of the house, and when they return, Tammy's with them. It's as if they know something's not right, as all of them stay glued to my girl as she takes the last empty seat at the table. I notice she inches her chair closer to mine.

Her dad opens his mouth, but Tammy stops him. "Nope, I get to ask the questions. But first, have you all formally met?"

"No," I say.

Pointing at her parents, Tammy says, "Meet Jeffrey and Brenda Turner. Mom and Dad, this is my boyfriend, Jason Donnelly, Jay for short."

Until she just mentioned it, it never occurred to me to ask Tammy what her maiden name was. I make a mental note to do a background check on them.

"So, why are you here?" she asks.

"Is that any way to greet your parents?" Brenda asks.

"Stop. Just stop. You haven't been my mom since I was eighteen. Now, one of you answer me."

"No need to be rude," Jeffrey says. "We saw you at the bar, and it seemed like you were in a pretty high position."

"And?" Tammy says.

"Well, we figured since you were doing so well, we'd come visit."

"But what about when I was struggling with my health? What about when my ex-husband served me with divorce papers while I was in the hospital? It didn't occur to you that I needed you then?"

"We weren't in a position to care for you then." Brenda says.

"Not even so much as a phone call. There were so many times when I needed someone to talk to, and I had nobody. I was so down that I really thought I was nothing more than a worthless piece of trash. It wasn't until this amazing man came into my life that I started to feel good about myself again."

I give her hand a reassuring squeeze under the table, I'm so proud of how she's handling this.

"Why don't you just cut to the chase and tell me what you want," Tammy says.

"You remember that we were scientists and had research grants, correct?" Jeffrey says.

"Of course I remember. It's why you were never around."

"Well, our research never produced any results. Eventually, the grants went away, but we continued with our own money. Unfortunately, we didn't fare any better. We lost everything." Jeffrey says.

Tammy jumps up from the table with such force that her chair falls over.

"Are you fucking kidding me? Are you actually here to ask me for money?" Tammy shouts.

"Yes," Brenda whispers.

"How dare you? You kick me out at eighteen. You move away, not telling me where. You're not there through some of the darkest times of my life. And now that you need money, you show up and try to disrupt my life? And I do mean try because I won't let you do it."

"But, Tammy -" Jeffrey begins.

"No. Remember what you said to me? You said I was an adult, and you had completed your job as parents. To me, that means that as of that moment, I was no longer your daughter. Not that I was even before then. Everything I learned in life and everything I am came from your parents, Brenda."

"It's Mom," Brenda says.

"No, it isn't. You lost that title when you said your job was done."

"But, darling, we're desperate," Jeffrey says.

"I. Don't. Care."

I hear Tammy's voice start to break. I stand up and fix her chair.

"Have a seat and relax," I say quietly.

She looks up at me, and I can see tears starting to form. I guide her into the chair.

"I think it's best that you two leave," I say.

"But what about our money?" Jeffrey says.

"Your money? I thought you didn't have money," Tammy says.

"We will when you give us some. We know all about your big win in Atlantic City, so don't pretend you don't have any."

My blood starts to boil, but I manage to keep it together.

"How dare you? I can't believe you've had someone spying on me. Wait, oh my god, is that why Martin keeps showing up?"

Jeffrey and Brenda look down at their feet.

"The last little bit we had left, we paid him to follow you. But that's over now."

"Do you realize that every time he approached me, he insulted me, made me feel like shit?"

"He didn't tell us his methods, and we didn't ask. We just wanted to find you."

"I have one more question. Is this why you sold Grandpa's Mustang, even though he wanted me to have it?"

"Yes," Brenda says. "And I've never regretted it once. Who cares about sentimental garbage when something's worth that much money?"

"That's it! I've heard enough. Neither of you has a caring bone in your body. I'm actually glad you were away most of the time. Spending time with Grandma and Grandpa ensured I didn't turn out like you."

"And like so many other things, that was a source of our disappointment. Our only child turns out to be this touchy-feely, normal human being. You could have done great things, but look at you. You're nothing," Jeffrey says.

That's the last straw for me, and I can't keep quiet any longer.

"Excuse me? The man who's here begging for money thinks he's better than the successful daughter who has it. I think you have that backwards. Your daughter is smart, talented, kind, caring, beautiful, and she's damn good in bed." I look over and give Tammy a wink. I couldn't help throwing that last one in. I may catch hell for it later, but the shocked look on her parents' faces is worth it.

Jeffrey opens his mouth, but I cut him off.

"Now, it's time for the two of you to leave. And you will never attempt to contact your daughter in any way. Is that clear?"

They both nod as they get up from their chairs. Jeffrey starts to head for the back door.

"I don't think so," I say. "You will not be seeing the inside of our house. I'll walk you out to your car."

"What about Tammy?" Brenda asks.

I glance back at her, and she shakes her head no.

"She needs to keep an eye on the dogs. Now, let's go."

We get to the driveway, and my blood's still running hot.

"I meant what I said back there. You will stay away from Tammy. She has a good life now, and you will not upset that. How on earth you could pull Martin back into her life after what he did to her is beyond me. How you could ignore your daughter when she was scared and alone in the hospital is beyond me. And then to come here begging for money, yet still manage to insult her, I just don't know what to say. Except for this. You're both scum, and you don't deserve a daughter like her."

Brenda starts to cry. I wave my hand as if I'm shooing a fly.

"Don't give me that fake crying shit. The only reason you're sad is because you're still broke. Well, too bad. I'm really starting to believe there's something to this whole karma thing."

I stand in the driveway, arms folded across my chest until I can no longer see their car. I grab my cell and dial Bruno.

"Hey, man, I need a favor. Can you run a background on Jeffrey and Brenda Turner? And please add them to the banned list for the bar? I'll explain later. And one more thing. I need updated security at home."

"Consider it done, boss."

"Thanks, man."

When I get out back, I see Tammy down by the garden with the dogs. I join her, and she falls into my arms. Her body quakes as sobs take over.

I sit and point at my lap. "Sit with me, butterfly."

She sits on my lap, and I pull her in close. I can feel her tears soaking my shirt as she sobs.

"All I want is to be able to take your pain away, but I don't know how."

"Yes, you do. This is how. Please, just hold me. That's all I need right now."

As if they sense something, all three dogs come lay quietly around Tammy, never taking their eyes off of her. It's at that moment that I realize something. Something I never thought I'd want again. But before I can think about that, I need to accomplish my first mission.

Chapter Eighteen

Tammy

I'm on my way to the Saloon to take care of this week's payroll when my cell rings. I get to a shopping center and pull in. I see a missed call from Mel, so I check the voicemail.

Hey, girl. Thought another girls night was order, but this time with a third. Allie. Call me when you can, and let's set things up.

I dial Mel's number, and she answers right away.

"Hey," Mel says.

"I was driving, so I couldn't answer. I'm definitely up for another adventure."

"Awesome. How about Friday? Allie said that works best for her, since unlike us, she's not a lady of leisure."

"Ha ha. Friday sounds good."

"You sound like you need it. Everything okay?"

"Could be better, but don't worry. It's nothing to do with Jay."

"Well, you can fill Allie and I in on Friday."

"Okay."

"See you then."

"Looking forward to it."

When I get to the parking lot at the Saloon, I see a familiar car. Son of a bitch. How dare they show up here? I get out of my car and start to head inside. I see Jeffrey and Brenda racing to catch up to me.

"Leave me alone," I shout before I open the door.

"I'm afraid we can't do that. We need money, and we're damn sure gonna get it," Jeffrey says.

I pull the door open and again shout, "Leave me the fuck alone!"

I hear boots, and in about two seconds flat, Bruno's standing next to me.

"Leave the premises immediately, or I will call the police," Bruno says, his voice stern.

"Go ahead. Call them. They'll take our side. This bitch owes us," Brenda says.

"Vinnie, out here now," Bruno calls out.

Vinnie, his second in command, joins us. "Please escort these two inside while I call the police. Do not let them out of your sight."

"Yes, sir."

Bruno dials the police, and a short time later, two police cars pull into the lot. I call Jay, and he races down here as well. The officers come inside and ask me what happened. As soon as I start talking, Jeffrey interrupts me.

"Sir, please be quiet until we get to you."

I fill the officers in on what happened at home yesterday as well as what just happened. The officer takes notes.

"Okay, sir," the officer says to Jeffrey, "now it's your turn."

Jeffrey recounts his version and finishes with, "So you see why this jerk is wrong. She owes us this money."

"The law disagrees. She's an adult and under no obligation to care for you. Unless you entered into a contract, and she breached that contract, you have no legal recourse. As far as your daughter, however, she does have some options. Do you wish to press charges?"

"No, I don't, Officer. I just want them to leave me, leave us, alone."

"Very well. This is your final warning. Please return to your vehicle and head away from the premises. And if we find you've returned, we will not hesitate to arrest you. You are officially trespassed from the property."

Jeffrey and Brenda storm out, and we hear them squeal their tires out of the parking lot.

"Thank you, officers," Bruno says.

"Of course. Please let us know if anything happens. We'll also try to make periodic drive-throughs to keep an eye on things."

Vinnie walks the officers out while Bruno briefs Jay on the whole event.

"Thank you for handling it so quickly, This woman is my life," Jay says.

"Of course, sir," Bruno says. He heads over and gathers up his team to fill them in.

"I can't do this anymore," I say.

"What, sweetie?"

"Bring all this drama into your life. It's not fair to you. You've been nothing but amazing, and all I am is a fuck-up."

"Please don't think that. You didn't cause this, they did. Baby, if you think for one split-second this is going to make me leave you, you're dead wrong. I meant what I just said to Bruno. You are my life. You and those three furry-butts."

I can't help but laugh as I picture the three wiggle-butts. I love those girls, and they sure do know when I need them most.

"Okay, but please, if it ever does get to be too much, I'll understand."

"Well, it won't. I want them out of our life, not you out of mine. Promise me you'll never forget that."

"I promise. I may slip sometimes, so you'll need to give me a swift kick in the tush when I do."

"Okay, but only a virtual kick."

"Fair enough. Oh, by the way, on a happier topic, Mel called me earlier. She wants a girls night with her, me, and Allie this Friday night. Is that okay?"

"You never need my permission to do anything."

"Oh, I know. I just wanted to make sure you didn't already have something planned for us."

"Nope, so enjoy! I'll see what Judd and Dane are doing. I promise no drunken calls this time."

"Good. We only help you with that once!"

"Oh, it's like that, huh!"

****

"Mel just pulled into the driveway!" I hear Jay shout from downstairs.

"Okay, just getting my shoes on, and I'll be down."

Grabbing my purse, I head out to the driveway. I see Allie in the backseat. I give Jay a kiss, which earns me giggles from the girls, then get in next to Mel. We all wave to Jay as we back out of the driveway.

"Anyone have a suggestion for tonight's outing?" Mel asks.

"I do," Allie says. "How about we relive being teenagers in the eighties. We could go to the mall, eat at the food court, then cruise the mall, ogling dudes."

"That sounds perfect," I say.

"I third that," Mel says.

"I do have to confess something," I say. "I've never done the mall like this."

"What do you mean?" Allie asks.

"When I was a teen, I didn't have friends. Do you remember when they used to have an art studio where you could pay a small fee and paint or draw? I was always there, alone. Or I'd be in the record store. I was never comfortable in the boutiques and clothing stores. Only the pretty girls went there. I tried once and had a *Pretty Woman* moment. They actually asked me to leave because it was embarrassing having me in their store."

"Oh, that's just awful. Well, this time, things will be different. And we're gonna have a blast!" Mel says.

And have a blast we did. We decided on salad for dinner, since most of the other food court restaurants are fast food. We ended up lapping each of the three floors twice. When we got to the boutique that had kicked me out so many years ago, I sat on the bench outside.

"Get that cute butt off that bench. You're coming in with us," Mel says.

"Yeah, we aren't gonna buy anything here, but we just want you to get the satisfaction of walking in, looking around, and walking right back out," Allie says.

They each grab a hand before I can decline, and they pull me up. We walk in, do a lap around the store and walk out. As we're leaving, I hear Mel say, "I wouldn't buy anything here. It's all cheap crap."

We're all in hysterics the second we leave the store. The laughter continues as we make our way to the exit where Mel parked. Everyone is staring at us, and for the first time in my life, I don't care. I've heard the saying *Laughter is the Best Medicine* countless times, but I never really bought into it. Maybe because I didn't have much to laugh about. Now, though, I get it and it's definitely true.

"Now that we've conquered the mall, what next?" Mel asks.

"We could go to my place and see what the guys are up to," I say.

"Good plan. Allie?" Mel asks.

"Thumbs up," Allie says. I notice a look between Allie and Mel, and I start to get nervous. I have flashbacks to the other girls pretending to be my friend and doing something mean to me. But that couldn't be happening again, could it? And if not, what was that look?

We pull into Jay's and my driveway, and see three guys doing a not-so-great job of hiding the fact that they've been up to something.

This should be a doozy!

Chapter Nineteen

Jay

Judd and Dane get here not long after the girls leave. Tammy has no idea that I had a hand in this girls night. Mel and Allie have specific instructions on how long to keep Tammy away from the house.

"Okay, what did you need our help with?" Judd asks.

I fill the guys in on the story Tammy told me about her grandpa's car.

"Why would her mom do that?" Dane asks.

"Trust me, you wouldn't ask that if you'd seen the things that happened recently. Her parents showed up out of the blue begging for money," I say.

"Wait, the same people who kicked her out at eighteen never to be seen again?" Judd asks.

"Yep. This girls night is multi-purpose. Besides picking up the car, it will help take her mind off of everything."

"How much does one person have to deal with?" Dane asks.

"I've been wondering that myself. But then I look at the fact that she's survived every single thing that's been thrown at her. That tells me she's destined for something great," I say.

"Hey, I saw a small glimpse of her artistic talent that night we played Pictionary. Maybe that's her true destiny. Well, that and spending the rest of her life with you," Judd says.

I can't help but smile at the thought of waking up next to her, next to my wife, every morning. Now that I've found the car, my next mission can start. But this one, I'm keeping under my hat for now.

"So, what do you need from us tonight?" Dane asks.

"Just to come with me. I'm going to need to drive the car back."

"You got it. Let's go. And hey if it needs a bath or anything else, we'll help," Judd says.

"Thanks, guys. I can't wait to see Tammy's reaction when she sees it."

We have about an hour ride to the home of the seller.

"So, how did you find the car and confirm it was the actual one her grandpa owned?"

"Bruno is a man of many mysteries. He was able to search using only the license plate number. That led us to the VIN number and the current owner. I found a box of photos among Tammy's stuff that had several pictures of the car, including the plate."

"Wow, that's amazing. I gather you didn't ask Bruno how he did it," Dane says.

"I figured it was best I didn't know."

When we arrive, I see the car sitting out front, and it's stunning. Judd and Dane wait in Judd's truck while I go knock on the door. An older gentleman comes to the door.

"Mr. Reilly?" I ask.

"Jason," he says.

"How did you know?"

"Oh, um, I remembered your voice."

I'm not so sure that's true, but no need to get off on a bad foot.

"You can call me Jay, Mr. Reilly."

"I'm Ed."

I hold out my hand, which he accepts.

"Would you like to see the car?"

"I would."

"Okay. One moment. Let me tell my wife you're here. I need her to find something."

"Of course."

After he returns, he walks me over to the car. Everything is pristine, and I'm so grateful that the car was sold to someone who took care of it.

"That your buddies in the truck?" Ed asks.

"Yes."

"They're welcome to join us."

I wave the guys over. They look the car over, and I can see the awe on both of their faces.

"My wife and I were moved by your story. We were, however, a bit on the fence about parting with it."

"I can appreciate that. The car is stunning. What made you decide?" I ask.

"Ah, here's my wife now. Jenny, this is Jay and his friends."

Mrs. Reilly smiles as she hands Ed an envelope, which he passes to me. I swear I can see tears in her eyes when she looks at me. I see Tammy's name on the outside.

"What's this?"

"We found this tucked inside the glove compartment after we bought the car," Jenny says. "You should read it."

"I don't know. It's addressed to Tammy. I feel like she should read it first. But could you tell me if it's a good letter or a bad letter?"

"I'll just say that her grandfather loved her very much."

"Thank you, Jenny."

I tuck the letter in my back pocket. As much as I'm tempted, Tammy should be the first to read this and make the decision who, if anyone, she wants to share it with.

"This letter is why we decided to let you have the car. We couldn't keep this car and this woman separated for one more day. Nothing is more painful than being separated from things, or people, that you love. Please, assure her we've taken good care of this treasure. We hope it brings her the peace and happiness she clearly deserves," Ed says.

"Thank you so much," I say. "What would you like for it?"

Mrs. Reilly whispers something in her husband's ear, and he smiles.

"We don't want any money," Ed says.

"That's kind of you, but I wouldn't feel right."

"We've had years of enjoyment from this car. We have more than enough for the rest of our lives. Instead, we have one humble request," Ed says.

"And that is?" I ask.

"For you and Tammy to come visit us from time to time. And of course, you must come in the Mustang."

"We can absolutely do that. Are you sure I can't pay you anything?"

"That's a dealbreaker."

"I'm so grateful. I can't wait to see Tammy's face when she sees it."

Ed hands me the keys, and I see sadness on his and Jenny's faces. I'm starting to have second thoughts about taking the car.

"Are you both sure you want to part with this car? You look upset."

"Oh, no, not at all. It's not the car," Ed says.

Jenny gives him a strange look, and he doesn't say another word. I shake off the strange feeling I have and get in. I start the car, and it sounds as good as it looks. I get out and shake Ed and Jenny's hands.

"Would you like me to call when we're planning to visit?"

"No need. We're always here. Just the two of us alone. Getting visitors always brings us joy," Jenny says. I see tears again.

"Very well. Expect a visit soon. Take care, and thank you again."

I drive over to where Judd's parked and wait for him and Dane.

"Hey, man, are you okay?" Judd asks.

"Of course, why?"

"You had a strange look on your face back there," Judd says.

"Since you mentioned strange, I have this strange feeling of familiarity here. Especially with Ed and Jenny. I've never been here, and I've never met them that I can recall, but there's definitely something."

I shrug my shoulders, and Judd and Dane don't say anything. That's definitely a better conversation to have with Tammy later. But not until after she's had a chance to enjoy her surprise. I notice something on the back floor when I'm about to get in. A box of eight tracks. I see one by Blondie, and I notice Tammy's name written on the label. I can't believe these are still here. I pop it in the player, which amazingly still works, and start the drive back, Judd's truck right behind me.

I'm grateful that I'm making the drive back alone. My mind is racing. Could Ed and Jenny be? No, knock it off. Focus on Tammy. She's what's important. But the feeling I had there. *Jay, turn your damn brain off and enjoy the ride.* Why did they really give me the car, only wanting to visit in return. Could they be? This continued until I pulled into the driveway and had Judd and Dane there to distract me.

"Dane, can you text Allie and let her know we're back?" I ask.

"Sure. How much time do you need?"

"Tell her to give us fifteen more minutes."

"You got it."

I pull the Mustang into the garage and give it a wipe down with a soft towel. I pat my back pocket where the letter sits. My plan is to wait until the others have gone home before I share that with her. I walk back to the driveway and shut the garage door, waiting for the big unveiling.

The three of us stand in front of the garage, waiting for Mel's car to pull into the driveway. I'm so excited for Tammy to get home that time is dragging and I keep looking at my watch.

"Calm down, man. Allie texted that they're on their way," Dane says.

"I know, but I just can't wait to see her face when I open the garage door," I say.

"Honestly, I can't either. It's so amazing that you were able to track it down."

I hear a car coming that sounds like Mel's. When I hear it slow, my heart starts beating out of my chest, and when I see Mel's car turn in, I can barely keep a straight face. I'm trying like hell not to give anything away.

"Hello, ladies," I say as Tammy, Mel, and Allie get out of the car and join us.

"Okay, what are you up to?" Tammy asks.

"Whatever makes you think I'm up to something?"

"I know that look anywhere."

"Fine you win. I have a surprise for you, but I guarantee that you will never be able to guess this one."

She bounces up and down, clapping. "I've loved every one of your surprises so far, so I'm excited to see this one."

"This is by far my best one yet. I know you'll agree. But before I reveal it, I need you to join me here."

She walks to the garage door and stands next to me.

"Now close your eyes. And please, no peeking. This is too important."

Mel and Allie start bouncing, too. I make sure Tammy's eyes are closed before I push the button on the remote to open the garage door.

Once the door is all the way up, I say, "Okay, baby, open your eyes."

Tammy opens her eyes, and her mouth drops. She doesn't move, doesn't speak, just stands there, eyes wide, mouth hanging open, and gazes at the Mustang. She doesn't even try to hold back tears and within minutes, her face is soaked.

"Jay. Is it...? Oh my god. Is it his? I mean the exact actual one he owned?"

"Yes, my love. I've had Bruno helping me track it down. Turns out, it was only about an hour's drive from here. So, I enlisted Mel and Allie to help get you out of the house while Judd, Dane, and I went to get the car."

"I'm speechless. You know how much this means to me."

"I do, sweetie. This has been my mission since you told me about it in Atlantic City."

Without warning, she flies into my arms and almost knocks me over.

"I will never be able to thank you enough for this."

"You already have. Your reaction is everything."

"How did you get them to part with it?"

"They were more than willing. They told me they got a lot of years of enjoyment out of it, and it was time for someone else to do the same."

"That's so sweet."

"So, how about we head home and let these two enjoy the car?" Mel asks.

"Thanks, everyone, for helping me tonight," I say.

After a big group hug, Dane and Allie, and Judd and Mel head home.

"So, when are you gonna take it for a spin?" I ask.

"Since it's getting dark, I'd like to wait until tomorrow. I want to be able to really see everything."

"Sounds good. For now, there's more we need to talk about. Let's head inside." I take the envelope Jenny gave me out of my pocket. Tammy and I take a seat on the couch. "I held some information back while the others were here."

"What?"

I hand her the letter. "This is the reason they decided to give us the car."

"You know, I just realized, I never asked their name."

"Ed and Jenny Reilly. They live about an hour away in a modest home. I have more I need to talk to you about where they're concerned, but this first. They found this in the glove compartment and just couldn't bring themselves to part with it after reading it."

"Did you read it?"

"No. I felt that you should read it first, and then decide if you wanted to share."

Tammy takes the letter out and opens it. I sit quietly while she reads. She has a soft smile on her face as she reads. I suspect that this time, her tears are happy ones. She finishes the letter and hands it to me.

"Are you sure?"

"Yes, please. I want you to."

The letter is written by her grandpa.

My dearest Tamara,
If you're reading this letter, I've completed my journey on this planet. I know you're devastated, but you will get through this. I hope your mother honors my wishes and gives you my car. But regardless, know that I am always with you. Every time you see a butterfly, that's me. I'll always be there looking over you.
I've always felt you were destined for greatness. Sure, you will likely hit some obstacles along the way, but your strength and resilience will overcome anything thrown your way. And I also believe there is a man out there somewhere who will love you and care for you in a way that only you deserve. You may not meet him right away. You may have to weed through some less than desirable men to find him, but I know you will.
I always cherished the time you spent with me working on the Mustang.

You were the daughter I always wished your mother was, and you were worth the wait. I love you more than anything.
My love always,
Grandpa

The words are so beautiful, and I now have an even better understanding of why Ed and Jenny did what they did. It's almost like he had the gift of predicting the future. I just hope I'm worthy of what he wanted for her.

"I'm glad my mom didn't know about the letter. She probably would have thrown it out."

"Me too. It was so beautiful. Grandpa was clearly a very wise man."

"He was. Now, you also mentioned you had more to say about Ed and Jenny. I'm ready to listen."

"Okay. But first, there's a secret I've been keeping. And I'm finally ready to tell someone."

Chapter Twenty

Tammy

"I knew you were a man of mysteries."

"This one is a big one. And it's one that I've truly never told a soul. Not even Mel."

"I'm ready when you are. And if it's not tonight, you know I'm okay with that."

"No, I need to do it. I've been carrying this for way too long."

I look at him, but don't say anything. There's a look of pain on his face, and I'm glad I can be here for him.

"I'm guessing you've noticed I haven't said anything about my parents."

"I have, but I didn't feel right asking."

"Thank you for that. There isn't much I could tell you anyway. I have no memory of them. My only childhood memories are the group home I spent my entire childhood in. I saw lots of other kids come and go being adopted or fostered, but for some reason, nobody wanted me. So I worked hard, graduated near the top of my high school class, and earned a scholarship to college."

"Oh, Jay. I'm so sorry."

"Thanks, sweetie. I always wondered who my parents were, and why they didn't want me, but I never had the courage to look them up. But tonight, something strange happened when I went to get the car."

"What happened?"

"There was something familiar about The Reilly's and their home. Like I knew them and had been there. But as far back as I can remember, I never was. There was also some strange looks between them and a couple awkward parts of the conversation."

"Oh my god, Jay. Do you think they could be your birth parents?"

"I know it probably sounds crazy, but maybe. Especially when I tell you what they wanted for the car."

"What did they want?"

"They wouldn't take any money. The only thing they wanted was a promise that you and I would visit them from time to time, in the Mustang, of course."

"Really? I can definitely see why you think there's that possibility then."

"So, I'm not crazy?"

"Not in my opinion. Could I ask you something? What was it like growing up in that environment?"

"For me, it was lonely. I was never abused or anything, but I was ignored. And sometimes, the other kids made fun of me. I was on the smaller side until I turned sixteen. I had my entire growth spurt. It's where my tough exterior came from. That was the only way I could survive. I always longed for a family, though I never shared those feelings out loud."

"If Bruno could find the car, do you think he could find your birth record?"

"I guess he could, but I'm not sure I want him to. What if I don't get the answer I'm looking for? What if I'm wrong and something terrible happened to my birth parents?"

"I understand. Is it better to know for sure, or is it better to believe what you believe and leave it at that?"

"Exactly. Maybe when we start visiting Ed and Jenny, we'll get some clues. Having you there gives me another set of eyes and ears. One favor, though."

"Anything."

"Please keep this between us."

"Without question. This is your story to tell when and if you want to."

"Thank you, baby."

****

On a warm, breezy, Sunday afternoon, we decide to take the Mustang and go visit the Reilly's. This will be our first visit since Jay picked up the car, and I'm looking forward to meeting them. Jay's been on the quiet side today. Not surprising after everything he told me.

I love the feeling of the wind in my hair as we drive. I have Fleetwood Mac blasting out of the eight track player as I sing along quietly. Jay usually joins me, but he's lost in thought. Luckily, he gave me the address, and I can use the GPS on my phone to get here, or we'd be lost right now.

I pull into the driveway and immediately get a sense of home. I see two people, who I presume are Ed and Jenny, sitting on the porch.

"We're here," I say quietly. "Are you sure you're up for this today?"

"Yeah, I am. Especially with you by my side."

"You know, I was thinking, too, if you were theirs, wouldn't your last name be Reilly?"

"Not necessarily. But it's still a big stretch that I'm even theirs."

"True. Let's do this."

We walk over to the porch, and we're greeted by a big smile from Ed, and an even bigger hug from Jenny.

"Ed, Jenny, this is Tammy," Jay says.

"It's a pleasure to meet you, dear," Jenny says.

"The pleasure's all mine," I say. "I can't thank you enough for reuniting me with my grandpa's car."

"You're very welcome."

"I agree with my wife. I'm impressed that you can drive a stick," Ed says.

"Grandpa taught me to drive in that car, so I've always been able to drive stick. Like he said, that way I'm prepared for anything."

"It sounds like he was a very wise man," Ed says.

"That he was."

"Come join us on the porch," Jenny says.

Jay and I follow her and take the two empty seats.

"May I bring you both something to drink?" Jenny asks. "I just made a fresh pitcher of diet iced tea."

"I'd love a glass," Jay says.

"I would, too," I say. "I'll come help you."

I follow Jenny inside while Jay and Ed wait on the porch.

"You have a lovely home," I say as I glance around the kitchen.

"Thank you. Would you be a dear and get four glasses down for me?"

"Of course."

"I usually ask Ed when I can't reach, but you're so tall, I figured you could help."

"I'm five foot nine."

"Wow. I never made it past five foot three."

"Well, I've always heard that good things come in small packages."

Jenny smiles warmly. "So, tell me, how did you and my - I mean Jay meet?"

My eyebrows shoot up, but I don't say anything about her almost slip. "I was waitressing in a bar, and he came in with his friends. We became friends first. I had a bad first marriage, and it took me a while to let him in, but he never gave up on me."

"He seems like a good man."

"That he is. When the bar where I worked went up for sale, and I thought I was going to lose my job, he stepped up. He had recently retired from his first job and was looking for a project. So, he bought the bar. Not only did I get to keep my job, but he made me second in command."

"Oh, that's wonderful, dear. Shall we rejoin the men?"

"Of course," I say.

I carry the tray with the glasses and Jenny carries the pitcher. After everyone has a glass of tea, we sit down to talk.

"So, Jay, tell me about your job," Ed says.

"After college, I was hired by O'Laughlin Consulting in their IT department. I worked my way up to the executive board as the head of the IT team. After the owner's nephew tried to use the company as his personal playground, I decided to take an early retirement. My investments and the salary I earned at the company gave me the freedom to do that."

"You sound very successful. What are you doing now?" Ed asks.

"It took me about a day to realize sitting around wasn't for me. So, the first thing I did was adopted two black labs from the local shelter. Then, an opportunity presented itself that I couldn't resist. I met Tammy when she was a waitress at The Full Moon Saloon. When the owner decided to sell the bar and retire, I decided to buy it."

"Tammy was telling me about that inside," Jenny says. "You're a very kind man."

"She makes it easy," Jay says, and I blush.

"He reminds me a lot of my Ed," Jenny says.

I see Ed shoot her a look. I'm not sure if Jay saw it, too, but he was definitely warning her not to say anything more. I'm starting to think Jay is on to something here. Ed and Jenny are definitely hiding something. But could it really be what Jay thinks it is? There sure are a lot of signs, especially after what Jenny said in the kitchen. Not to mention, sometimes when I look at Ed, I see signs of Jay.

We visit for about another hour before deciding it's time to head home. I help Jenny take the glasses into the kitchen. She gives me a big hug. "Please don't be strangers."

"We'll definitely be back."

"And please, take good care of Jay."

"I promise."

After we finish our goodbyes, Jay and I walk back to the car.

"You wanna drive this time?" I ask.

"If you wouldn't mind, I'd rather you drive. I have some thinking to do."

"Of course. And if you feel you want to talk, let me know."

He nods, but doesn't say a word. I plan on telling him what I observed when he's ready to talk. I can only imagine the jumbled mess inside his head right now. I give his hand a squeeze before I start the car and begin the drive home. He doesn't say anything until I pull into our garage and park.

"Can we go sit out back with the dogs and talk?"

I give him a big hug. "Of course, I'll go get them."

Chapter Twenty-One

Jay

I'm sitting on the bench down by the garden when I see three furry flashes run by, followed by my angel. She sits next to me and takes my hand in hers. This woman always knows exactly what I need. She sits quietly, waiting for me to be ready to talk.

"Baby, can I ask you what your impressions were as a fresh set of eyes?"

"Of course. I think you may be on to something. When I went inside to help Jenny get the iced tea, she had a small, verbal slip. I didn't feel right pointing it out or pushing her on it. She was asking me how we met. She asked 'how did you and my - I mean Jay meet'. Now, of course, that could have been a coincidence, and I probably would have brushed it off if not for everything you told me."

"Anything else?"

"Well, a few times when I saw Ed smile, I could see you in his face. Now again, that could be my imagination after what you told me. I don't know."

"I don't think it was. I'm more convinced than ever. While you were inside, the questions Ed was asking me made it sound like he was trying to get to know a long-lost relative."

"Hey, I just thought of something. Couldn't we get your file from the group home?"

"Yeah, I guess we could. I'm just not sure I'm ready yet."

"I understand. I don't think there's any right or wrong time where this is concerned. Like you said, you need to be ready. And you know I'll be here when you are."

"I'm just so angry right now. How the hell could they give me up? I'm their son, and thanks to them, I grew up without parents."

"I understand."

"Oh, you do, huh? Like hell. You knew who your parents were, and yeah, they weren't the best, but you had your grandparents. So, don't tell me you understand what I've been through."

Shit.

I look at Tammy and see the hurt look on her face. I give her a hug.

"I'm so sorry, baby. I shouldn't take this out on you."

"No, you shouldn't, but sometimes you just need to vent. Please know I don't take it personally. Just please don't make a habit of it. And you're right, I don't understand your specific scenario, just the emotions."

Out of nowhere, I start shaking, overcome with emotion. Within seconds, I'm sobbing. Tammy throws her arms around and holds on tight. Even as I soak her shirt with my tears, she doesn't move. I've never been this overcome before, and part of me feels embarrassed, like I'm less of a man.

"I'm so sorry. I can't imagine how much this just damaged my masculinity in your eyes."

"What are you talking about? You think this makes you less of a man? Well, I assure you, you couldn't be more wrong. In fact, to me, it makes you more of a man. And it deepens my faith in our relationship. If you're able to be this vulnerable with me, I know I can trust you."

"Baby, I'm not sure I'd survive this without you."

"That's not true. You wouldn't be in this situation if not for me."

"What do you mean? This isn't your fault."

"If not for me telling you about the Mustang, you wouldn't have gone looking for it. And then you wouldn't have found them. You put it behind you, then I come along and messed everything up."

"Okay, now it's my turn to tell you that you couldn't be more wrong. None of this is your fault. You didn't give me up with no thought to how it would affect me."

"True, but I can't help but feel responsible. So, let's both agree that we will be here for each other and we will get through this, like we get through everything."

"It's a deal."

****

I've been able to distract myself with work, and of course Tammy and the dogs, but a small part of my brain remains focused on what to do about my parents.

Then, everything changes. Tammy heads in early one morning to get payroll done, and while she's gone, I head over to the local jewelry store. I think I look at every single engagement ring before I find the perfect one. I hide the little velvet box in a secret compartment in my truck and head to the Saloon.

"Hey, doll face, you almost done?"

"Yeah, just submitting the last time sheet for processing, then I was planning on coming home."

"Okay, I'll follow you, and we can drop your car off. I need you to go somewhere with me."

"Of course. Can I ask where?"

"I'm ready to see my file at the group home."

****

A little while later, we pull into the parking lot of the group home where I grew up. I stand outside the door for a few minutes, Tammy's fingers linked through mine. When I finally work up the courage, we walk inside and approach the reception desk.

"May I help you?"

"Yes ma'am. I grew up here as a child, and I'd like to see my file."

"One moment please."

The receptionist disappears behind a door marked For Personnel Only. She returns with a man who approaches Tammy and I.

"I understand you wish to view your file. My name is Art, and I'm the current director here at the home."

"It's a pleasure to meet you," I say. "My name's Jason Donnelly. Would it be okay if my girlfriend joins us?"

"Of course. Follow me, please." Art leads us to a small conference room. "Please have a seat, Mr. Donnelly. I'll be right back with your file." After he identifies me, he returns a few moments later and places a file on the table. "I'll give you two some privacy," Art says and walks out of the room.

I slide the folder over to Tammy. "Will you look at it first?"

"Are you sure? I'm willing, but I want you to be sure."

"Please, baby. I need you to do this for me."

She strokes my arm and says, "Of course." Tammy opens the folder and starts reading. She closes the folder a little while later and slides it over to me. "I think you should look at this."

"Does it tell you who my birth parents are?"

"Yeah. And it also explains why they gave you up. You really need to read it."

I open the folder as Tammy slides her chair closer. I feel her arm circle my waist. As I suspected, Ed and Jenny are my birth parents. What I didn't expect was why they gave me up. And what I'm reading breaks my heart.

Reason for surrender:
Jennifer and I do not believe we have the means or the talent to raise a child. We've been told countless times that we're inferior in every way. We cannot, in good conscience, bring a child into that environment. Our child deserves nothing but the best of everything. Sadly, we're not the ones who can give him that. Please promise that he'll keep up with his studies so that he can achieve the success he deserves. And most important, please make sure he's raised to be kind and caring.

"Oh, Tammy."

"I know."

"At first, I hated them for abandoning me, but after reading that, how can I?"

"I agree. It makes me sad that people made them feel that way. Made them feel their only option was to give you up. Even with the little bit of time we spent there, I think they would have been great parents. Why do people have to be so mean?"

"Are you still talking about them?"

"I am, but not just them."

"No wonder you and I ended up together. We needed each other."

"No, we'll always need each other."

"I love you, Tammy."

"I love you, too, Jay."

"Well, shall we head out? I'm going to see if Art will let me make copies of what's in the folder before we go."

"Okay."

We head back to the reception desk, where Art stands waiting for us.

"Thank you," I say. "Would it be possible for me to have a copy of the contents of the folder?"

"Of course. Give me a couple of minutes, and I'll be back."

After we have an envelope containing all the information, we head out and get back in my truck. I sit for a few minutes before I start the truck.

"What's next?" Tammy asks.

"There's two things I need to do, just not sure which first."

"If I may ask, what?"

"I want to tell Mel and Judd the whole story, and I want to go back and tell Ed and Jenny we know."

"There's no doubt which one will be easier. I know neither will be easy, but let's face it, telling Mel and Judd will be easier."

"It will. Would you mind if we head there now?"

"Not at all. Should we call first to make sure they have time for a visit?"

"Good idea. Would you mind calling Mel?"

I grab my cell and dial Mel's number. She lets me know they have no plans today, so we head over.

"Mel said they'd be out back, so to head back when we arrive."

I pull into their driveway and grab the envelope. We walk to the backyard and join our friends at their patio table.

"Hey guys," Mel says. "Tammy sounded serious on the phone. What's going on?"

"I don't even know where to start, but I have to tell you something."

After I fill Mel and Judd in on everything, I end with, "I'm so sorry I never told you."

"Don't be silly," Mel says. "That couldn't have been easy."

"I remember you saying something felt familiar the night we went to pick up the car. Did you have any inkling that's what it was?" Judd asks,

"A little bit, but then I thought I was crazy. But after talking to Tammy and having our first visit together, it definitely seemed less crazy."

"For the record, I never thought it was crazy," Tammy says.

"I can't believe you went through your whole life not knowing who your parents were," Mel says.

"Trust me, that's not always a bad thing," Tammy says. "Now, not in Jay's case, of course."

"But yeah, we know about yours," I say.

"So, are you gonna tell them?" Judd says.

"I am. I just don't know how. It was hard enough coming here to tell you two."

"Do you think they have any suspicion?" Mel asks.

"Based on something Tammy said, I do," Jay says.

"What was that?" Mel asks.

Tammy fills Mel in on what Jenny said that day in the kitchen. Mel nods her head up and down and says, "Yeah, definitely sounds like they know."

"How was it going back to the home?" Mel asks.

"Not much has changed. The current director made me a copy of my file," I say, putting my hand on the envelope. "There's a note inside that explains why they gave me up."

"May I - Wait, sorry, that's personal," Mel says.

"It's okay, ask me," I say.

"What was the reason?" Mel asks.

I take the paper out of the envelope and let Mel and Judd read it. Mel gets teary-eyed, and Judd puts an arm around her. When they finish, she looks at me.

"How sad that people made them feel that way," she says.

"That's why I can't hate them. And it's why I want to tell them."

"I'm so glad he has you to help him through this," Mel says to Tammy.

"Me too. The universe brought us together for a reason," Tammy says.

"I hate to cut our visit short, but it's been quite a day," I say.

"I understand," Mel says.

****

We pull into our driveway and see a familiar car.

"I'm pretty sure they know," I say.

I park in the driveway and approach Ed and Jenny, or should I say Mom and Dad's car. Suddenly feeling awkward, I grab Tammy's hand and squeeze. She looks over at me, then turns to Ed and Jenny.

"Welcome," Tammy says with a warm smile.

Jenny, tears in her eyes, races to me and gives me a hug.

"Art called and let us know someone came in to see your file. It was part of our agreement, that we would be notified if it was viewed. He wasn't allowed to confirm it was you, but we knew," Ed says.

"I hope you're not upset, but I had to know," I say.

"We're not upset. You had every right. We're honestly surprised you didn't check before now," Jenny says.

"I never really thought about it. It was something I wanted to put behind me. But after that night when I came to get the car and felt like I knew you, I got curious."

"Where do we go from here?" Ed asks.

"To be honest, I have no idea," I say. "But I would like to get to know you both."

"And we want to get to know you," Jenny says. "Tammy, too, of course."

"Um, what should I call you?" I ask. "Using your first names doesn't seem right anymore."

"What do you want to call us?" Jenny asks.

I hesitate for a moment until I feel Tammy squeeze my hand.

"Can I call you mom and dad?"

Tears slide down Jenny's face and Ed gives me a hug.

"We'd be honored," Ed says.

I walk over to Ed and Jenny, my parents, wow, that sounds weird, and pull them both into a hug.

"I'm so glad I found you, Mom and Dad."

"And you're not mad?" Mom asks.

"At first, I was mad and I was hurt, but then I read your reason. There's no way I could stay mad. But it does make me sad that other people made you feel that way."

"We weren't yet married when we had you. Our parents are the ones who made us feel that way. We were both still in high school, and we messed up their plans for us," Dad explains.

"We really wanted to keep you, but they convinced us we'd never be able to handle it. We were too young and stupid to fight back, and we've regretted it every single day," Mom adds.

"Well, the past is the past. Now, we move forward, and we make up for time lost," I say.

Noticing that Tammy's been quiet, I turn to ask her something, and I realize she's not there. I never even noticed her leaving. I see the front door is now open, so I peek inside.

"I hope we didn't upset her," Mom says.

"If I know her, she was trying to give us some privacy. She's so kind and thoughtful. Would you like to come inside and see our home? I assume you're comfortable with dogs," I say.

"Oh, we love dogs," Dad says.

We get inside, and the dogs are curled up in the corner, but Tammy's not with them. I call up the steps, but no response. I look out back, and she's not there either. That's when I notice her purse and her keys aren't where they usually are. I look out in the garage and the Mustang's still there, but her car is gone.

"Where's Tammy?" Mom asks.

"I'm not sure, but we have an app to track our vehicles, so I can find her."

I pull up Tammy's car and see that she's stopped at our favorite park. I look at my parents, unsure if I should go after Tammy or stay here with them.

"Let's go get her," Dad says.

"Okay, let me just run upstairs and grab something."

We load the dogs into my truck, and my parents follow me in their car. When we arrive, I see Tammy sitting on a bench just gazing out at the lake. I leash up the dogs, and we walk to where she's sitting. Her back's to us, so she doesn't see us approach, but Sadie gives us away. She turns, and I see a beautiful tear-stained face looking back at me.

"Butterfly, what happened?"

Chapter Twenty-Two

Tammy

"Why did you follow me? You don't need me anymore."

"What are you talking about?"

"Come on, Jay. You have your family. Don't get me wrong, I'm so happy for you that you found your parents, but now you have all the family you need."

"Baby, if you think I no longer need you, then you don't know me at all."

"Sure. The girl who was rejected by her first husband and whose parents only tried to come back into her life now because they're broke. You don't need a broken down piece of garbage like me."

"May I?" Jenny asks Jay

He nods yes, and Jenny sits down next to me. She shoos the men away, so they take the dogs for a walk around the park.

"Sweetheart, why would you say those mean things about yourself?"

"Because it's the truth."

"Not from what I've observed in the short time I've known you. Why don't you tell me what happened?"

Like I did with Jay, I feel comfortable around Jenny. He must have gotten that trait from her. And before I can stop myself, I've tell her the entire story about my medical issues, what Martin did to me and what my parents did to me. Jenny held my hand the entire time, the way a mother should treat a child. Not at all like my own mother,

"You sure have been through a lot. None of which makes you what you said. It makes you a survivor. Look at you now. My son adores you. I see it in his eyes every time he looks at you. And just think, had you not come into his life and told him about your grandpa's Mustang, he may never have found us. I truly believe there's that one person out there for each of us. Ed's mine, and Jay is definitely yours."

"Thank you for saying that. And please accept my apology for running out. I just got overwhelmed back there."

"No need for apologies. After hearing your story, I completely understand. I think I see the men. Should we let them come back?" Jenny winks at me.

"I guess we have to." We both laugh as she waves Jay and his dad back.

Jenny and I sit quietly while we wait for them. As they get closer, I'd swear I can see a cat who swallowed the canary look on each of their faces.

"I think they've been up to something," I say.

"Me too. Time to grill them," Jenny says.

"What were you two chatting about?" I ask Jay and his dad.

Jay looks down at his feet. "I hope you won't be mad, but I was filling Dad in on some of your history."

"I'm not mad. I filled your mom in."

Ed sits down next to me. "I'm so sorry that people felt it was okay to treat you like that. I'm glad you and Jay found each other," Ed says.

"Believe me, so am I," I say.

All of a sudden, I hear a sharp bark from Sadie and wonder what has her upset. A familiar voice behind us gives me that answer.

"Well, well, well, if it isn't piggy piggy."

"Please, Martin, leave me alone."

"I'm afraid I can't do that. Your parents still need money, and I'm here to collect."

"I think I've been perfectly clear that they aren't getting anything from me."

153

"I really don't give a shit. If you give them money, I get a cut, so the only thing I care about is getting that money."

"Fine. You win. But I'm not discussing it here. If you want my terms, come with me to the dock."

"Babe, are you sure?" Jay asks.

I turn and wink at him. "I've never been more sure of anything in my life."

I walk down to the dock, Martin in tow. I look back, and he has the biggest shit-eating grin on his face. *Yeah, enjoy it now dickhead. You may think you won, but you're about to find out what a loser you are.*

"Okay, bitch, let's hear your terms."

I move closer to him, and his smile gets bigger. Good. That will make this moment even sweeter. I glance over and notice that Jay and his parents are watching from the end of the dock.

"Here you go," I say.

Before he gets a chance to say another word, my hands fly to his chest, and I shove with all my might.

Splash!

Martin's arms flail around as he realizes he's now in the lake. I'm laughing so hard, tears are rolling down my face.

"What the hell, bitch?" Martin shouts.

"You listen to me. I'm done with this. I will never give my parents so much as a penny."

"Well, at least help me out of here!"

"What did you always tell me? I believe it was along the line of me being worthless and lazy. Well, since you feel that, guess I'm gonna have to prove you right. I'm just too damn lazy to help."

I turn on my heel and walk off the dock. Jay and his parents are in hysterics, and a crowd has gathered. A woman I've never met walks over.

"Can I ask you who that was?" the woman asks.

"My ex-husband. He was horrible to me, and that was long overdue."

"How did that feel?"

"Amazing. Freeing. Like I'm finally at peace."

"Thank you for giving me the courage to do the same. I just called my ex and asked him to meet me here."

"Well, congratulations and good luck," I say.

"Damn, woman, I've never been prouder," Jay says.

"Not my finest moment, but it felt good."

"He had it coming."

Jenny and Ed are still laughing. They both give me a hug, and the four of us, and of course, the dogs, head out of the park.

"Would you like to join us for dinner?" Jay asks.

"Oh, we wouldn't want to put you out," Jenny says.

"Not at all. I love cooking. Please join us," I say.

"Well then, we accept," Jenny says. "But I have a condition."

"What condition?" Jay asks.

"That Tammy let me help. I've always wanted a daughter to cook with, so please let me cook with you."

"I'd be honored," I say.

Jenny's face lights up. I look at Jay, and he looks so happy. That makes my heart so happy.

"I need to run to the store to grab a few things, so I'll meet you all at home," I say.

"May I go with you?" Jenny asks.

"I would love that."

Jay and his dad load up the dogs in his truck while Jenny and I head to the store. After I pull into the parking lot, we head inside.

"Can I ask you what happened with Martin that made you that upset?"

"He was never very nice to me. He always made snide comments about my weight before I lost it. Worst of all, though, while I was in the hospital the second time, he served me with divorce papers. That forced me to find in-home help until I was strong enough to be on my own. And he hasn't let up, even after I've lost all the weight. I finally just had enough, and, well, I pushed him into the lake."

"I must say, it was quite the site. His arms were flailing everywhere as he went in."

"I enjoyed it a little more than I probably should have."

"Oh, I don't think so, dear, after what you told me."

"You're so sweet. I wish my mom had been more like you."

Jenny doesn't say anything, and when I look over, she's got tears in her eyes. I give her hand a squeeze.

"You know, if you and my son get married someday, I'll be proud to call you my daughter-in-law."

"Thank you so much. That's definitely something that's been on my hand, but I certainly don't want to put any pressure on him."

"I understand. So, what's on the menu tonight?"

"I was planning on grilled chicken Caesar salad. I make my own lower sodium dressing."

"That sounds delicious."

After we finish up at the store, we head back to the house. Jay and his dad are out back enjoying a beer while the dogs play. Jenny and I get to work preparing the meal. She works on the salad while I go out back and cook the chicken on the grill. I head back inside when it's done, and Jenny assembles the salad while I make the dressing. I haven't felt this kind of joy since the last time I cooked with Grandma.

I get plates and silverware together, which Jenny carries out back. I bring the salad out, along with the loaf of garlic bread I bought.

"What can I get everyone to drink?" I ask.

"Dad and I still have beer left," Jay says.

"I'd like iced tea, please," Jenny says.

"That sounds good. I'll be right back."

I return with two glasses, and a pitcher of diet iced tea. After pouring a glass each for Jenny and I, we pass the salad bowl around. The men insist that Jenny and I take ours first since we prepared the meal. Such gentlemen. I see more and more traits that Jay has in common with his dad.

As usual, I made too much food, but I'll send some home with Jay's parents. The men insist on cleaning up, so Jenny and I walk around the yard and play with the dogs.

"Thank you for letting me help you today. It meant so much to me," Jenny says.

"I feel the same way. Since my mom was the way she was, I only had Grandma to do that stuff with. Now, I'm lucky enough to have you."

We walk a little more as Jenny admires the garden. She takes my hand in hers as we walk, and I feel this sense of calm wash over me.

"This garden is so beautiful."

"It is. Jay had a few bushes out here, but I added a lot of the flowers after I moved in. I love the variety of colors. I think all those months spent in medical facilities with their plain white walls got to me, so I try to add a little bit of color anywhere I can."

"Not to mention, my son tells me you're a very talented artist."

"He's so sweet."

"He is indeed. I'd love to see some of your work sometime."

"I have a portfolio here. Would you like to see some now?"

"Oh, wow, I'd love to."

We're about to head inside when I hear the back gate open.

"Hey, Tammy, you out here?" I hear Mel call out.

"Hey, Mel."

Mel stops when she sees me with Jenny. "Oh, I'm so sorry. Jay told me to come out here."

"It's fine. Come join us. This is Jay's mom, Jenny. Jenny, this is Mel."

"It's a pleasure to meet you," Mel says.

"How do you know my son?" Jenny asks.

"We started at O'Laughlin around the same time and became instant friends. He was like a big brother to me. We worked our way up to the executive board together," Mel says.

"And she gave me my first real friend, and I'll always be grateful," I say.

The men join us out back. Jay and Judd are laughing.

"Oh, I can only imagine what Ed may have said," Jenny jokes, eliciting a laugh from Mel and me.

I walk to the garage to grab two more chairs, and Mel follows me. "So, what do you think?" she whispers.

"She's so sweet and Jay's so happy."

"Then I am, too."

Mel grabs one of the chairs, and I grab the other. We take them to the table and join the others. We spend the rest of the evening talking, telling stories, and just having a blast. Time flies, and I happen to notice on Jay's phone that it's almost eleven. The dogs are all curled up in a furry ball, sound asleep.

"This is the latest we've been out in I can't remember how long," Ed says. "I think we better head home."

Jay and I walk them inside while Mel and Judd wait with the dogs. I pack up leftovers for them and put them in a bag. We walk them out to their car, and after a round of hugs, they get in their car and head home.

Jay and I rejoin our friends in the backyard. Of course, I have to fill them in on the incident in the park earlier. Mel and Judd can't stop laughing.

"I'm so glad to see how happy this has made you. Just please, promise me you'll be careful," Mel says.

"I will. I know it seems like I'm getting caught up, but you know I never completely let my guard down. Well, with one exception."

Jay strokes my cheek, and I turn to goo inside.

After they're gone, we bring the dogs inside. I didn't realize how exhausted I was. I think the adrenaline of the day was keeping me going, but now, I can barely drag my ass upstairs. After a quick kiss goodnight, I don't remember another thing until hot breath times three panting in my face wakes me up.

****

A couple months have passed since Jay found his parents. We've had regular visits, but I am happy to note, he does remain cautious. They've definitely given us no reason to doubt them, but we just can't be too careful nowadays. I hope it's just that we're being overly cautious, as I would hate to see anything fracture their relationship.

Jay's down at the bar checking in with the security team when the mail arrives. Among quite a few normal sized envelopes, there are two big packets. I flip them over and both of them are addressed to me. I squeal when I see who they're from. I know what the big packet means, and I'm so excited. I can't wait for Jay to get home.

He has no idea I did this. I was so afraid that I'd be rejected, that I didn't tell anyone. I get the dogs back inside, lock up, and jump in the Mustang. I have to fight hard not to break every speed limit from here to the bar. I park, grab the envelopes and skip inside. I see Jay talking to Bruno, so I bounce up and down on my heels waiting for him.

"What's got you so excited?"

"I kinda did something."

"Something secret?"

"Yeah. And only because I was afraid of what the response would be."

"And what was it?"

I wave the envelopes around. "I applied for admission to art programs at Franklin & Marshall as well as the Pennsylvania College of Art & Design."

"And you got the big envelopes! Oh my god, baby, you did it! But what made you decide?"

"Your encouragement. I never told you what my secret dream has always been. I never told anyone because I thought it was unattainable. But you gave me the self-confidence to start the pursuit."

"Well, tell me, what's your dream?"

"To own an art studio. I would have my own work on display. I would also provide a place for students to practice and show their work. I might even consider teaching classes at some point, But first, I want to get my formal education and degrees."

"Look at you, Butterfly. I'm so damn proud of you. We are going out tonight to celebrate. And you will need the outfit I got you in Atlantic City, as I plan to take you somewhere fancy." Jay takes out his cell and dials. "Mel, can you keep the dogs overnight for us? I'm taking Tammy to Philadelphia overnight to celebrate. We'll fill you in when we get home." He pauses a moment. "Great, thanks." Jay runs up to his office. He comes back down, a huge grin on his face. "We're spending tonight in the Presidential Suite at the Four Seasons in Philadelphia."

"But, that's so fancy."

"Nothing but the best for a future world-renowned artist."

"I wouldn't go that far."

"I would. The sky's the limit for you, baby. Look at how much you've spread your beautiful wings, my precious Butterfly. I do have one request, though."

"And what's that?"

"I get to commission your first piece of paid artwork. And you better come up with your special signature, as I'm gonna want it signed."

"I already have one. It's hidden in every one of my drawings and paintings."

"Then when we get home, I'm hiring you to paint for me. In fact, I do believe there's a very large empty room upstairs. I never knew what I wanted to do with it, but I do now."

"Oh my god, no way. I can't let you do that."

"Sorry, you get no choice in the matter. We're going shopping to get whatever you need, and we're doing it this weekend."

"Duly noted. Thank you so much for being so supportive."

I sit down for a minute, taking everything in. I can't believe my dream is actually on the horizon. But now I have a new, brief moment of panic.

"I need help with something else."

"What, babe?"

"I'm not sure which school I want to pick."

"Well, we'll have time to talk about it on our flight tonight."

"Our flight? I thought we were just going to Philadelphia."

"We are, but I arranged with Mr. O'Laughlin to borrow the company jet. He was more than happy to lend it out."

"Have I ever told you how amazing you are?"

"You have, but more importantly, you show me. Every. Single. Day."

Chapter Twenty-Three

Jay

Tammy's not the only one with secrets and surprises. There's another reason I'm taking her here tonight. I know she thought I set this all up while I was just in my office, but that would never have been possible. I was actually already planning this. Her news about art school was a total coincidence. I'm going to make what I hope is another dream of hers come true.

I sent her to Mel's to drop the dogs off so I could pack without her seeing. I tuck the little velvet box inside a pouch inside my suitcase. Dinner is going to be something she never forgets, but not because of the food. Once she gets home, she packs, then we both grab a quick shower and get dressed in our fancy clothes.

A limo picks us up and takes us to a private airstrip. Tammy looks like a princess as she's helped up the steps and onto the plane. I follow, and we sit down in two luxurious leather reclining seats. We buckle up while the pilot readies the plane for takeoff. It takes about forty minutes to get to a private strip near the hotel, where another limo waits to take us the rest of the way. We have enough time to check in and relax a few minutes before we head down to dinner.

I arranged for a private tasting menu experience for us, and every bit of food is delicious. Tammy was a little nervous to try some of it, as it was food she's never eaten, but I made sure everything was prepared in a way that made it safe for her to eat. After dinner and dessert, we're sitting and sipping on the most delicious coffee I've ever tasted.

Our personal waiter comes in with a bottle of sparkling white grape juice and two glasses. He quietly places them on the table and leaves. Shortly after, the music starts. *Lucky* by Jason Mraz and Colbie Caillat. I can't help but wonder if Tammy's starting to figure things out. I stand and walk to her chair, helping her stand and face me.

Taking her hands in mine, I say, "Tammy, the love of my life, tonight I celebrate your amazing success as you begin your true journey. And please know that journey will always have me by your side. But we're also here to celebrate something else, the actual reason I planned this little getaway."

Butterflies take flight in my stomach. I stop and take a deep breath. After slowly exhaling, I continue.

"You've breathed new life into me, given me something I didn't even know I was missing. And while I didn't think I could love you more, everyday, that love increases, and I can't bear the thought of life without you."

Judging by the tears welling up in her eyes, she knows now. I reach into my pocket and pull out the small velvet box that matches her beautiful eyes.

As I open it and show her the ring, I ask, "My beautiful Butterfly, will you do me the honor of becoming my wife?"

She sits and stares at me, then the ring, then back at me. Her mouth is open but no sound is coming out. I get nervous, thinking I went too far when suddenly, her brain switches back on, and she shouts, "Yes. Oh my god yes!"

I put the ring on her finger, and she holds her hand in front of her beautiful face.

"Oh, Jay, it's stunning. I don't think I've ever felt this happy."

"Me either. I love you so much."

"I love you, too."

A few more songs play. I hold her tight against me as we sway to the music. I picture us dancing like this on our wedding day, all of our friends and family watching us, celebrating with us, and I feel myself getting choked up. This woman has completely rocked my world.

We sit down and drink a toast to our engagement and Tammy's future career before we head back to our room.

"Now, my love, it's time to *really* celebrate," I say.

"Mmmm, I like the way that sounds."

I walk behind her and unzip her dress, letting it fall to the floor. My mouth waters when I see her standing there in nothing but emerald colored lingerie and heels. She's stunning. I run my fingers down her spine, and she shivers. I lay her hair over her shoulder and shower her neck with kisses. Her soft skin tastes and smells delicious and I can't get enough of her.

"Mmm, Jay, feels so good," she murmurs.

I unhook her bra and remove it, gently caressing her breasts. This goddess, so sexy. I slide her panties down, and she steps out of them, kicking her shoes off as she does. I turn her around so she's facing me and take every inch of her creamy white skin in my eyes.

"So fucking beautiful."

Usually, she gets shy when I stare at her, but something's different tonight. Sliding her hands down her body, she asks, "See something you like?"

Watching her touch herself sends me soaring, and I rip my clothes off. I scoop her up in my arms and carry her to the king size bed in our suite. Her giggles as I lay her down make my dick do a happy dance, and I can't wait to be inside her.

I lay back and say, "Please, baby, come ride me. I need to watch you while we make love."

"Good. I love being in charge. Then I get to control the rhythm."

"My god, Butterfly, are you the same woman I first met?"

"No, and that's because you helped free me. Now, less talking and more lovemaking."

She climbs on top of me and slowly slides her sweet, wet pussy down my cock. All I can do is growl. She's so hot and wet, and it feels so fucking good. I watch as she sits up, her hands on her breasts as she writhes on my dick. She leans back, giving me an incredible view of her body. I feel her body quake as her moans get louder. She explodes around me, sending me over the edge, and I empty inside her.

Gently rolling her onto her back, I climb on top of her, my dick immediately hard, and easily slide inside her. Slowly, tenderly, wrapped in each other's arms, we make the most passionate love I've ever felt. After I empty a second load into her, I grab a soft towel and clean her. Lying next to her, I slide my fingers inside her, stimulating her g-spot until she squirts all over my hand. Her chest rises and falls quickly as she comes down.

"I've never done that before. It felt unlike any orgasm I've ever had. You're an incredible lover," she whispers.

"And just think how many firsts we're going to experience together, especially becoming husband and wife."

"Oh, Jay. I honestly wasn't sure I'd ever marry again after Martin, but then you came along. And now, I can't wait. The thing I'm most looking forward to is wearing a wedding dress and veil for the first time."

"The first time?"

"Yeah," she whispers. "Martin said I was too fat for a wedding dress. He made me wear a housecoat."

"Okay, I think he needs another dip in the lake."

Tammy laughs, but it's forced, and I can see the pain on her face.

"Well, this time, you'll be in the most beautiful gown ever created."

She smiles at me, but it quickly fades.

"What's wrong?"

"Um, do you think Mel would be my matron of honor?"

"Of course she would. She adores you, and I know she'll be honored."

Tammy sighs. "Sorry, I know I shouldn't be thinking about these types of things tonight, but I still get moments of fear."

"Never apologize. Just always do what you did and talk to me. We can work through anything together."

She looks at me and this time her smile stays. We curl up together under the covers and Tammy's quickly asleep. I sneak out of bed without waking her, shut off all the lights, and rejoin her. She mumbles something I can't make out and lays her head on my chest.

****

We're still in the same position we fell asleep in when we wake the next morning. Tammy wakes up a little after me. She yawns and stretches her arms out to the sides. "Oh, I'm still naked," she giggles.

"Mmm, yes you are. How about breakfast in bed?"

"Oooh, yeah, baby, give me some of that sausage."

"Damn, woman!"

I start to move on top of her, but I stop when I hear, "No, no, no. On your back. Now."

I growl. I love a woman in charge.

"Middle of the bed," she commands.

She hovers her sweet pussy over my aching cock. Barely taking the tip inside, she teases me. "Fuck, woman." I try to thrust up inside her, but she pulls herself up.

"I'm in charge. You get my pussy when I say you get it."

Holy shit. This woman!

She lowers herself and takes a little more inside. I see her rolling her hips so her clit's rubbing my erection. Her moans are music to my ears. I want nothing more than to feel every bit of her around me. But she's being a naughty little tease this morning. I put my hands on her bottom and squeeze lightly.

Her moans are getting louder as she rubs, and in one quick motion, I'm all the way inside her. She's riding me harder than ever before. Screaming with pleasure, I feel her soak my dick as she orgasms. Her body is shaking like a leaf and she's pressed against me. She keeps fucking my cock over and over, each orgasm more intense than the last. Somehow, I've managed to hold off and I'm damn glad I did.

"I wanna try something," she whispers.

"Anything, baby."

"I wanna taste you."

Before I can respond, she climbs off of me, gets on all fours, and lowers her sweet soft lips on my cock. Watching her head bob up and down is the sexiest fucking thing I've ever seen.

"Oh god, Butterfly," I cry out as I empty my dick into her mouth.

She gets on her knees, and as she gazes into my eyes, swallows every last drop of me. Holy. Fucking. Shit.

"Baby, do you have any idea how hot that was?"

"Mmm, yeah. That's why I wanted to do that for you. And I really really liked it, so you will be getting that again. But only if you behave."

"Yes, ma'am," I tease. "Now, I hate to cut this short. I'd rather stay in bed all day, but the limo will be here in about an hour."

"And we definitely both need showers. And to save time, I think we should shower together."

"Only in the interest of saving time, I agree." Tammy laughs and gives me a light swat on my ass.

After we get home and pick up the dogs, we spend the rest of the day naked in bed.

Chapter Twenty-Four

Tammy

"Any idea where the girls are taking you tonight?" Jay asks while I'm getting ready.

"Not even the smallest hint. The only information I was given was what to wear."

"Oh, before I forget, and this is a totally different topic. When you bounced into the bar and saw me talking to Bruno, I had him run full background checks on my parents just to make sure they were on the up and up."

"And?"

"They were. I'm relieved, as I'm not sure I could have handled anything else."

"I'm glad, too, but I think it made sense to do it. You just can't be too careful these days."

I'm putting the finishing touches on my makeup when I hear the doorbell.

"I got it," Jay says and heads downstairs.

I come down a few minutes to catcalls from Mel and Allie.

"Let's go. Our chariot awaits," Mel says.

Jay escorts the three of us outside. Parked in our driveway is a pink party bus that looks like someone poured *Pepto-Bismol* all over it. I see a disco ball and colored lights dancing inside. I have a feeling this is going to be a fun night.

The limo pulls up in front of the new Hollywood Casino in Morgantown. We head inside, and Mel leads us to the casino's theater. We're greeted by an usher when we get to the door.

"Tickets, please," he says.

Mel grabs her phone and pulls up the tickets. The usher scans all three and gives us wristbands.

"You're in the VIP first row. Show your wristbands to the usher in that area. Enjoy the show, ladies."

I still have no idea what we're seeing. Mel and Allie are being brats, and they won't tell me. I ask the usher, Judy, when we get to our seats, but I see Mel shake her head no, so the usher won't tell me.

"Our sweet friend just got engaged, and this is our gift to her," Allie says with a wink.

Judy nods and smiles. "I think your friend will be most pleased. Congratulations on your engagement," she says to me.

"Thank you," I reply.

We take our seats, and a few minutes before showtime, I see the word hunks appear on the curtain hiding the stage. I know for sure now that I'm definitely going to enjoy tonight! The lights go down in the theater as the curtain starts to open revealing seven of the most delicious men I've ever seen, besides Jay, of course.

Mel and Allie start hooting and hollering, and I decide to throw caution to the wind and join in. After a couple of songs, the lead dancer, Max, brings a chair to the center of the stage. Grabbing a microphone, he stands at the front of the stage and says, "I understand we have a future bride here tonight."

I wonder what lucky girl that is. I'm sure it's someone young and hot. And then the panic sets in.

"Tammy Foster, get your cute butt up on this stage. Mel and Allie want you to have a *really* good time tonight."

I look over at my friends, who are now on their feet cheering me on.

"Either you go on your own, or we drag you up there," Mel says.

"You deserve this, girlie," Allie adds.

"Oh, what the hell? I do," I say.

I get up from my seat and walk to the stage. Max helps me up the stairs and walks me to the chair. I sit down, and all seven of the dancers surround me. Max grinds against me, and my two knucklehead friends are going bananas. I whisper to Max, and he grabs the microphone.

"Tammy tells me Mel and Allie are feeling left out."

He grabs two more chairs and motions for them to join me. The three of us are having a blast on stage. After another couple songs, we head back to our seats to enjoy the rest of the show. Afterwards, we hit a poker table. The men at the table, thinking we're a bunch of bird-brains, start mansplaining poker to us. We play along, but after about five hands, they realize we know what we're doing, and they all end up busting out. We collect our chips and head over to the cashier's booth.

Mel texts our limo driver, and we head outside to wait for him. Some of the guys from the table try to follow us, but security stops them when Allie alerts them. A guard stays with us until our driver picks us up.

"Oh my god, thank you both so much," I gush. "That was so much fun. Do the guys have any idea where we were?"

"Oh yeah, I cleared it with Jay," Mel says.

"I'm so proud of you for going up on stage," Allie says.

"I wasn't gonna, but I decided, why not live a little?"

"Well, it was great to see," Mel adds.

"Where to now?" I ask.

"I figured we'd work up an appetite, so we're heading to dinner," Mel says.

The limo takes us to John J. Jeffries restaurant in Lancaster. While we're waiting for our food, I say, "I need to ask you both something. And it's perfectly fine if you say no."

"Of course, ask away," Mel says. Allie nods in agreement.

"Will you be my bridesmaids?"

"Oh, Tammy, I'd be honored," Mel says, her voice breaking as she answers.

"I would love to," Allie says.

"I decided I didn't want a maid of honor. I love you both so much, so I want you both with the same title."

"You are so sweet," Allie says.

Mel nods as tears slide down her cheeks.

After dinner, the limo takes us back to Jay's and my house. I see Judd and Dane's trucks in the driveway, and I can hear talking from the backyard. We walk back and join the guys.

"So, did you ladies have fun tonight?" Jay asks.

I look down at my feet as my face heats up.

Jay laughs out loud. "Babe, it's okay if you did."

I still can't bring myself to look at him. Why am I suddenly so embarrassed?

"Okay, Mel, spill it," Jay teases.

"Let's just say she had quite a night. But I can honestly say that not one of those dancers held a candle to any of you."

"Awww, thanks," Judd says.

"And of course, this one," Allie says pointing at me, "had us in tears at dinner."

"How?" Dane asks.

"She asked Mel and me to be her bridesmaids," Allie says.

"That's great. Jay asked Judd and I to be his groomsmen," Dane says.

That leads to a group hug. I love that I've found this amazing family, after so many people let me down.

"So, I hear you gave someone a bit of a soak," Judd says.

"I probably shouldn't be proud of that, but it felt good.

Allie and Mel are looking at me.

"Um, forget to tell us something?" Mel asks.

"The other day, Jay and I were at the park with his parents. Martin showed up and was being his usual self. So, I lured him to the dock and shoved him into the lake."

Mel and Allie jump up and down, clapping.

"We're so proud of you," Allie gushes.

"Yes, we are," Mel says.

A little while later, our friends head home. Jay and I make sure the dogs have done their business then we head inside to bed.

****

"Jay, are you in the middle of anything?"

"No, what's up?"

"Come up to the studio. I need to show you something."

I have a cloth covering the easel. When Jay walks in and I turn the easel toward him.

"Are you ready to see the finished painting?"

"I had no idea you were that close."

"I wanted to surprise you."

I slowly lift the curtain, and Jay's jaw drops as his eyes light up.

"You're truly so talented. The painting is so life-like, I'd swear it was a photo. You did an amazing job capturing the personalities of the dogs. And us, standing there, holding hands, watching the dogs! Incredible. I love the small butterfly on my shirt, along with your initials. Why did you use TD instead of TF?"

"So, the painting would have what my initials will be after we get married.

"I love it, baby. The initials, of course, but most importantly, the painting. No way you aren't getting an A on that!"

"Thank you so much. I'm so happy with it. Once it's finished being graded, I'll be able to bring it back home. You get to decide where you want to hang it."

"I'm leaning toward the living room. I want everyone to see it as soon as they come into the house."

I feel my cheeks heat up, but I still have a big smile on my face. "Thank you for supporting my dream."

****

I can't believe we're only a week away from the wedding. Mel and Allie helped me pick out the most beautiful dress. Mel's been hiding it at her house so Jay doesn'tn't see it. I'm glad we decided to have a small wedding in our backyard. The saloon will be closed and certain members of our staff will be working here for the night.

With the managers we put in charge at the saloon, I've been free to spend less time there. I ended up enrolling in Franklin & Marshall's art program, so Jay and I will be delaying our honeymoon until the semester break.

Classes have been going well. I could live without the electives, but they want well-rounded students. The art classes, however, are amazing, and I've had a lot of positive comments from my professor. Our final project for the semester is a work of our own choosing, so I decide to use the painting Jay wants me to do.

I'm up in my art studio, which turned out beautifully, working on the piece, when I hear a knock on the door.

"Come in."

"How's it going, babe?"

"Wanna see what I have so far?"

"If you're okay with that."

"Of course."

He walks around to my easel and looks. "Oh my god, it's more beautiful than I could have imagined."

"I still have a long way to go."

"I know, but the picture of Sadie is breathtaking. I can't wait to see the other dogs."

"I plan on adding them first. Then, I'll put us in. I haven't exactly decided what I'm going to do with us yet, but I know I'll get inspiration."

"I have no doubt. You're incredible."

"Thank you. I think I'm good for today."

We head downstairs and grab some dinner, then head out back with the dogs.

"Anything left we need to do for the wedding?" Jay asks.

"I don't think so. The night before, Allie and I will be staying at Mel and Judd's house. We'll get dressed there in the morning."

"Yeah, Judd told me, so he and Dane will come here. Can I ask... How involved do we want my parents to be?"

"Well, that's up to you."

"Well, I would like to do a mother-son dance, but will that be too hard for you?"

"Not at all. Look, just because my parents are who they are doesn't mean you shouldn't give your mom that honor."

"You never stop amazing me."

"I plan to spend the rest of our lives doing that."

"Me too, Butterfly."

****

The day before our big day is here. Mel and Allie pick me up in the morning, and we head out to grab any last minute stuff we need. We're in the grocery store grabbing some snacks for our movie night pajama party. We turn the corner and come face to face with Martin.

"Oh look, it's Piggy Piggy. You two are so cute. Why the fuck are you friends with her?"

"Fuck off, asshole," Mel says.

"Didn't learn your lesson in the lake the other day?" I ask.

"Oh, you just think you're so damn cool now that you have pretty friends. Well, guess what, they just feel sorry for you. And I feel sorry for Jay. He must have lost one hell of a bet to be stuck with you."

I stand there, not saying a word. Mel and Allie just watch me.

"Aww, is the piggy gonna cry?"

"ENOUGH! I'm not a fuckin' pig!"

My raised voice draws a crowd, and someone asks Mel what's going on. She fills them in, and a murmur goes through the spectators.

"And just what are you gonna do about it, you fat pig?"

Something snaps inside me, and without a word, I pull my arm back and thrust my fist dead center into his face.

He goes down like a wet sack, holding his nose in his hands, screaming. "You broke my nose!"

"Yeah, good! Serves you right for serving me with divorce papers when I was in the hospital!"

That elicits a gasp, and then cheers out of the crowd. I hear a bunch of "serves you right" and "you go girl" coming from the crowd. Mel grabs her cell and takes a picture of him writhing on the floor. She sends a text to Judd with the picture and a caption that says, "Look what Tammy, aka Rocky Balboa, just did." Judd texts back laughing emojis and says they're from him, Jay, and Dane.

We finish our errands and don't find anyone else to punch, so we head to Mel's house. We all get in our jammies while Mel orders pizza. I don't normally eat it, but I decided to make an exception this one time.

We each eat a slice, then settle in to start our eighties John Hughes movie marathon. After the second movie, we set out our sleeping bags and continue our marathon. None of us has any idea which movie we fell asleep during, but we wake up the next morning still in sleeping bags on Mel's living room floor.

After a light breakfast, we start getting ready. Mel and Allie get my hair and makeup done. They help me into my dress, and I feel like a princess. The dress has white lace covering white satin from the waist down. The lace features butterfly patterns, as does the veil. The bodice is form fitting without being uncomfortable and is the same satin that's on the bottom. Since no one can see my feet under the dress, I wear ballet slippers for comfort.

After the girls get my veil in place, they get into their bridesmaids dresses. I wanted navy blue, which they were both excited about. They each have a floor length satin gown, just a simple design, but still stunning. They do each other's hair and makeup. I try to help, but they won't let me.

"This is your day," Mel says.

"What Mel said," Allie adds.

We're just getting downstairs when the photographer arrives. He takes us to Mel's back yard for our photos, then heads over to my house to get the guys. We head back inside, waiting for the limo to pick us up. Mel walks out back to make sure they keep Jay outside until I'm safely stashed in the den. Allie heads back upstairs, but Mel hangs behind.

"Are you okay? You seem a little sad," Mel says.

"I am. Not about the wedding, well not Jay. But I'm sad not having a father to walk me down the aisle."

"I understand. I was in the same boat. So, I held my head up and marched down that aisle alone."

"How did you do it?"

"Because I knew with Judd, I'd never be alone again. You have that with Jay, so that's your focus."

"Thanks, Mel," I say, giving her a big hug.

"It's time," Allie yells down the stairs.

"Let's go get you hitched, woman," Mel says.

She squeezes my hand and makes her ascent up the stairs. We're each coming in from around the side of the house. When I come up the steps and get outside, my jaw drops when I see who's standing there.

"I can't believe you're here!" I squeal as I race into the arms of my former boss, Nick.

"You didn't think I would miss this, did you? Jay called me after he mailed the invitation. He didn't want me to mail my RSVP so you would be surprised."

"Why are you out here instead of with the other guests?"

"Jay had a special assignment for me. Shall we?" Nick holds out his arm and I link mine through his.

"Are you sure you want to do this?" I ask, knowing instinctively what the big assignment he was given is.

"I was so honored when Jay asked me. I couldn't wait for the day to arrive. I never had a daughter, as you know, so to be able to do this for you is a highlight of my life."

I smile as we start our walk around the side of the house. I keep my eyes glued to Jay's face as he sees me. His jaw drops as I walk in, and I smile when I see Judd give him a pat on the back and whisper something to him. When we reach the front, Nick gives my hand to Jay and gives me a hug before taking his seat.

Chapter Twenty-Five

Jay

W hen I see Tammy and Nick come around the corner, my knees go weak. She's breathtaking, and all I can do is stand there, mouth hanging open.

Giving me a pat on the back, Judd says, "You are one lucky man."

After the officiant pronounces us husband and wife, I give Tammy a kiss that lets her know what I plan to do to her later. I'm tempted to send everyone home and take her to bed, but there will be plenty of time for that later.

Before we walk out, I say. "I have a special wedding gift for my beautiful butterfly."

Judd hands me my guitar, and I start strumming another of Tammy's favorite Jason Mraz songs, *If It Kills Me.* By the time I'm done, tears are streaming down her cheeks as she throws her arms around me.

Our officiant announces, "For the first time in public, I'm honored to present Jason and Tamara Donnelly."

We walk out, followed by Mel and Judd, and Dane and Allie. The guys join me in the house to get the dogs. Tammy's smile widens when she sees them. Each of the three dogs has a veil that looks like mine.

We all head down to the garden. The photographer gets my parents and Nick to join us. While we're getting our photos done, the cocktail hour starts. Waiters carry trays of hors d'oeuvres. After the photographer takes every combination of photos under the sun, we're finally free to join our guests. Nick's wife was sweet enough to make a couple plates of goodies for us, which we all chow down.

Our DJ, Zane, turns on our entrance song, *Boogie Wonderland*, by Earth, Wind, & Fire and The Emotions. "It's time to introduce our guests of honor. First up, we have Tammy's escort, Nick."

Nick struts in like John Travolta's character in Stayin' Alive.

"Please welcome the parents of the groom, Ed and Jenny Reilly."

My parents do their best attempt at some disco, and they look adorable.

"Now we have our bridesmaids and groomsmen. Please welcome Judd and Mel Walker, and Dane and Allie Bryant."

Our four goofball friends dance like Daryl, Kevin, and Oscar did to the same song on one of Tammy's and my favorite episodes of *The Office*.

"Last, but absolutely not least, Jay and Tammy Donnelly!"

We channel our inner Jim and Pam as we dance our way in and join our friends.

"And now, it's time for our groom to dance with his mother."

I can't help but notice the sad look on Tammy's face as she stands with our friends. Hopefully, my next surprise will help with that. Mel and Allie each take one of her hands, and some of that sadness disappears. After the mother-son dance is done, the DJ grabs his microphone again. "And now, Jay has another special surprise for his bride."

Another song starts and Nick walks out to the dance floor. He walks over to Tammy and says, "May I have this dance?"

She nods and joins him on the floor.

When they finish, the DJ grabs the mic again. "And now for our final dance before dinner. Jay and Tammy are going to enjoy their first dance as a married couple."

Jason Mraz and Colbie Caillat's *Lucky* starts, and we hold each other tight as we move to the music. I give her another deep kiss, and a round of cheers goes through the crowd. Damn this woman tastes so good.

When the song ends, we take our seats at the head table. We're the first ones served. While the rest of the guests are served, Judd makes a toast.

The DJ plays some soft music as we all eat. Once the tables are cleared, it's time for the party to really begin. Everyone hits the dance floor, and there's nothing but smiles all around. As we're dancing, I grab my wife's hand, and we walk around to the front of the house.

"I needed a moment alone with my bride."

"And just what do you plan to do with me?"

I pull her in tight, my hands firmly planted on her sexy little ass. I crush my lips to hers, leaving her no doubt how much I crave to be inside her tonight. She moans into my mouth as her tongue explores with such vigor I can barely control my dick. A throat clear interrupts our passion.

"Excuse me, lovebirds," Mel teases. "Everyone was looking for you."

"I just needed to get my sexy wife alone for a minute."

Mel gives us each a big hug, and we walk back to the party. I love seeing the friendship that's developed between Mel and Tammy. Allie too. The six of us have fun whenever we're together. We rejoin everyone on the dance floor.

As it reaches ten, guests are starting to filter out, and by eleven, it's just the six of us, my parents, and Nick and his wife.

"Thank you so much for inviting us. It was an honor to be part of the ceremony," Nick says. "We have a mid-morning flight tomorrow, so we're going to head out now. We love you both."

After a round of hugs and handshakes, they head out front, and we hear the car back out.

"I think we're going to follow suit. This was a lovely wedding, and we're so glad we could be here," my mom says.

"I have to agree," Dad says. "We wish you both the best, and we look forward to our next visit."

Tammy and I walk my parents out and wait until they're out of the driveway before we rejoin our friends.

"You two have quite a job ahead of you tomorrow," Judd says.

"And we couldn't be happier," Tammy says.

My always generous wife decided that for anyone planning on giving us a gift, she would prefer a bag of dog or cat food instead, so we could make a donation at the shelter where we adopted Lorelei and Sookie. And our guests really came through. Very few people only brought one bag. Tomorrow, we'll load up the back of my truck and make the drop off.

"If you need extra truck space, let me know," Judd says, referring to the dog and cat food.

"Same here," Dane offers.

"Thanks, guys," I say. "I'll call tomorrow if we need help."

Our friends get ready to head out. Allie and Dane hug us, followed by Mel and Judd.

"Thank you all so much for helping make this day even more special. Allie and Mel, I can't find enough words to thank for how you've made Tammy feel. After so many people let her down, seeing the three of you together is heart-warming," I say.

"She's helped me just as much," Mel says. I know she's referring to the strained friendship between her and Lexi.

"I adore both of them," Allie adds. "Just always make sure you have bail money ready when the three of us are together," she jokes.

"And guys, I was a nervous wreck today. I wanted everything to be perfect for my gorgeous wife, and you both helped keep me calm."

"Tammy deserved nothing less than perfect, and we were happy to be part of it," Dane says.

"Now, get that gorgeous lady upstairs and rock her world," Judd says.

We all laugh, but that's exactly what I plan to do as soon as they're gone. We all walk out front. After another round of goodbyes, our friends head home. Tammy and I walk to the front door. I open it, but I make her wait before going inside. I scoop her up and carry her into the house. Her arms are around my neck as she weaves her fingers through my hair. My dick loses its battle, and I nearly tear a hole in my pants. We don't even make it to the bedroom.

I pull out the couch-bed and walk back over to her. I remove her veil and lay it on the chair. I unzip her dress, and she steps out of it. All she's wearing now is a sexy white lace bra and panties. She may look like an angel, but I know there's a sexy devil under that lingerie waiting to take all of me inside her. And I have a special treat for her, if she's willing to try something new.

"Let me see you finish stripping for me, my sexy goddess."

I watch in awe as she unhooks and removes her bra. Her panties are close behind, and finally, her cute ballet slippers. I can barely contain myself as I watch her standing there naked. Damn, she's fucking gorgeous.

"Baby, I wanna try something new tonight."

"Mmm, what?"

"Get that sexy little body on the bed. I want you on all fours."

"Oh, Jay," she murmurs as she does what I tell her. I walk over and rub her ass. So fucking sexy. I get on the bed behind her. I run my hands up and down her back as she moans. I position her so I can slide my dick inside the sweetest, hottest pussy I've ever felt. She growls as she takes me hard and fast. There's something so primal fucking her like this.

"Oh god, so fucking good!" I shout as I fill her sweet pussy. I grab a towel from the powder room and clean her up. Now, it's time to drive her wild.

"On your back, my sexy wife. And get those legs spread wide."

I love how she no longer gets embarrassed and shy to show me her body. She meets my gaze and smiles at me. I crawl up the bed until we're face to face. I give her a kiss so hot she growls into my mouth. I've never wanted anything as much as I want to taste that sweet pussy. I glide my tongue down her body until I'm hovering over my favorite part of her body, after her generous heart of course.

I take my fingers and spread her wide. She keeps her eyes locked on mine, and it's so damn sexy. I lower my head and slowly swipe my tongue between her folds. My tongue moves slow and hard, and she starts to writhe beneath me.

"Harder, baby. It feels so fucking good!"

"Tell me what you want me to do."

"Oh god, Jay, please suck my clit. Hard. Make me scream."

It doesn't take long, and her body is shaking hard. She cries out, but I don't stop.

"Oh, Jay, so good, please!. I wanna explode over and over. Fuck, oh fuck, oh Jay!"

I start sucking on her clit again, even harder than before. Her body is writhing, bouncing off the bed as she keeps exploding. Her arms are tight around me, and every part of her body is quaking. I slide my fingers inside her and find her g-spot. I stroke it hard and feel her soak my hand. Her body bucks as she comes hard.

"Holy! Fucking! Balls! So! Fucking! Good! Must have your cock inside me now. Please, Jay, fuck me hard and fast."

She's so wet. I slide inside her easily. She grabs my ass, trying to pull me in further. Damn, this woman's insatiable, and I wouldn't have it any other way. She matches my thrusts. Nothing on earth feels more incredible than being inside this woman.

She looks into my eyes and says, "I love you, my sexy husband."

"Oh god, I love you so much," I growl as I empty inside her again.

Totally spent, I collapse next to her and pull her close. We're both soaked in sweat and plenty of other fluids. Chests heaving, we hold each other tight, celebrating our first night as Mr. and Mrs. Donnelly. That has such a nice ring to it. I kiss her softly, and she sighs. Within seconds, she's sound asleep. I lay there for a few minutes watching the beautiful butterfly who made all my dreams come true sleep.

****

The next morning, we load up my truck bed until it's full. I call in Judd and Dane, and we barely get all of the dog and cat food, along with the other goodies, loaded. Once we do, we head down to our local shelter. Our friends wait while Tammy and I go inside. I recognize Piper from when we adopted the labs.

"Mr. Donnelly, Miss Foster, welcome. How can I help you?" Piper says with a big smile.

"Actually, it's Mrs. Donnelly now," Tammy says.

"Oh wow, congratulations!" Piper exclaims.

"My beautiful bride and I asked for donations instead of gifts for our wedding. Do you see the three trucks parked out front?" I ask.

"I do," Piper says.

"Our guests did not disappoint us. The beds of all three trucks are

181

full of dog and cat food as well as some toys and other goodies. We're here today to donate everything," Tammy says.

"Oh my god. Let me grab Carly."

Piper returns with Carly. She gives Tammy and I a hug, and we all walk outside. Carly and Piper's eyes go wide when they see everything we have.

"If you can drive around back, I'll grab a few staff members to help unload," Carly says.

"Absolutely," I say.

Tammy and I get in my truck and head out back, our friends in tow. Three of the workers come out, each pushing a large flat bed cart. We fill up all three carts, and the workers take them inside. Once they unload them and return, we finish unloading. Carly takes all six of us inside to show us the storage area and how full it now is.

"I can't thank you enough for this. You've already done so much. With the economy, donations have been down, so this will really help us out by shifting some funds to other things."

"And thank you to your friends, and of course, all your wedding guests for making this possible," Piper adds.

After we're done, the six of us go grab lunch, then we all head home. Tammy and I are sitting out back, watching the dogs play.

"It seems strange sitting here in a quiet backyard after the party that happened here last night," Tammy says.

"The night we took flight together, my Butterfly."

She looks at me and smiles that same smile that hooked me the first time I saw her.

Epilogue

I 'm standing in the staging area. I can't believe I made it to this day. I adjust my cap and gown for the three-thousandth time. My magna cum laude cord is in my hand, waiting for the professor to place it around my shoulders. I hear the graduation march begin, and the procession starts. I'm walking with the other art students, as they have us grouped by our major. I scan the crowd as I walk to my seat. I spot Jay and his parents, Judd and Mel, Dane and Allie, and Nick sitting there.

When they announce the art major, we all rise, and I hear loud clapping and shouting from my friends and family. I walk to the stage, and when it's my turn, I hand my name card and honor cord to the professor.

"Tamara Lynne Donnelly. Congratulations." The professor places the cord around my shoulders and hands me a scroll representing my diploma. Another round of cheers, along with cell phone camera flashes from my cheering section follows me across the stage and back to my seat.

After the ceremony, Jay takes the group out to dinner. We have a blast together. Only Jay knows my plans for opening an art gallery. I was thinking about announcing it tonight, but I decide to wait until it's ready for its grand opening. We found a perfect place for it, and we've been working hard to get things ready. There will be the art display portion, plus several small studios for classes and for people just to come in and practice. I also plan on having a place where people can purchase supplies at a reasonable price.

Now that the semester is over, we can finally take our honeymoon. I know everybody likes all these fancy resorts and stuff, but not us. We decided to go to our favorite place. Jay booked a week at the Hard Rock Casino in Atlantic City. We have a blast spending time on the beach, doing some light gambling, getting pampered at the spa, getting a romantic couples massage, and of course, plenty of smoking hot sex. I can't get enough of this man.

When we get home, the workers we hired are done with the gallery, and all that's left is for us to plan the grand opening. One wall features the work I did as part of earning my degree. I do plan on enrolling in a Master's program down the road, but I want to get the gallery established first.

Our first night is going to be by invitation only. We invited our friends and Jay's parents. I also head down to my alma mater and speak to the professor I had in my senior year, Professor Watson.

"Hello, Tammy. It's wonderful to see one of my top students back."

"Thank you, Professor Watson. That's an honor, coming from you."

"What can I do for you?"

"I'm having a grand opening of my brand new art gallery and school next week. I thought maybe some of your students would like to attend. The first night is invitation only."

"That would be wonderful. I would love to attend myself and bring my top five or ten, depending on how much space you have. I'd love to be able to show them a real-life example of how they can use their degree."

"I can definitely accommodate ten plus you. I have the invitations with me. I'm happy to write them out if you give me the names."

"Tell you what, you can write mine, and I'll do the others once I get a chance to review everyone's progress and decide which students deserve the honor."

"That sounds perfect."

I pull out the box and count out eleven cards and envelopes. I fill out Professor Watson's and hand her that along with the ten blank ones.

"I can't wait to see what you've done."

"Thank you so much for all of your help and encouragement."

"You're so gifted. You made it easy for me."

We shake hands, and I head home. I fill out the rest of the invitations and get them in the mail. I can't wait to see who calls me squealing first. My friends are so sweet. Mel, Allie, and I have a monthly girls night where we compare notes and dish about our men. If they heard some of the stuff we talked about!

****

Opening night arrives. Jay and I arrive early to make sure there aren't any last minute things that need our attention. Everything is perfect so we relax a bit before the big opening is scheduled to start. Bruno sent us two members of his team to keep an eye on everything, or more specifically, to make sure nobody unwanted tries to enter. After that day I punched him at the store, I haven't seen or heard from Martin or my parents, but you just can't be too cautious.

Judd, Mel, Dane, and Allie arrive first. After they greet us, they walk around and look at my art on display.

"Oh, sweetie, I just can't get over how talented you are," Mel says.

"I'm so proud to say I know you," Allie adds.

"Right, when you're a famous artist, we get to tell everyone we're close personal friends," Mel adds.

"Awww, you two. I love you both so much."

As I'm standing with Mel and Allie, the men are standing off to the side. I look over at Jay, and he just stands there gazing at me. Damn, I love my man so much. His parents come in next. His dad gives me a hug and joins the other men.

"Congratulations, doll," my mother-in-law says. "This is so amazing." I see Jenny walk over and hug Jay before she and my father-in-law walk around and look at everything. I didn't tell them, but one of the pieces is a painting I did of the two of them with Jay at our wedding.

Jay's mom comes back, tears in her eyes, and says, "Thank you for the lovely portrait you did from the wedding. It's beautiful."

"You're very welcome," I say.

"Congratulations, Tammy," I hear a voice behind me say. I turn and see Professor Watson with a group of students.

"Thank you so much, Professor. Welcome, everyone. Please feel free to take a look around. I'm happy to answer any questions you may have."

"Class, you all have your assignments, so go ahead and get started when you're ready," Professor Watson says to her students.

The class spreads out and starts looking at all the work on display. I make the rounds in case anyone has questions until Jay stops me.

"Baby, watching you like this, I can't tell you how proud I am. You're such an incredible woman. I've heard nothing but positive comments about your work, and all I can think is that's my wife!"

"None of this would be possible without you."

"Wrong. None of this would be without *you*, Butterfly. Never forget that. You're the one with the talent, the drive, the fight."

"Maybe so, but you're the one who gave me the courage to make all of my dreams come true. For that, I'll love you forever." I put my arms around his neck and give him a kiss that he'll never forget.

The End

Acknowledgments

Cover Model Photographer: Jean Woodfin
Cover Model: Daniel Rengering
Proofreading and Editing: Melony Carter-Alexander
Cover Design Carter Cover Designs
PA Team: Carxander Publishing

About the Author

Samantha Michaels was born in 1973 in the small town of Abington, PA and was raised and still lives in Hatboro, PA (both suburbs of Philadelphia). She is married to her high school sweetheart and they have a rescue dog, a beautiful Black Lab named Holly.

When she's not writing or working at her full-time job, she enjoys watching her Philly sports team (hopefully) win, listening to heavy metal/hard rock music, Texas Hold Em, reading, and spending time with friends and family.

Her love of reading began at a young age, thanks to her mother and Sesame Street. Her mom read to her constantly, and by three years old, she was reading on her own, and hasn't stopped. This eventually turned into a love of writing.

To learn more:

Website

Newsletter

  BB

Also by Samantha Michaels

www.ingramcontent.com/pod-product-compliance
Lightning Source LLC
Chambersburg PA
CBHW020958180626
46814CB00003B/1148